Digital ISBN: 978-0-473-68948-3
Kindle ISBN: 978-0-473-68949-0
Print ISBN: 978-0-473-68947-6
                      978-0-473-68951-3

The Magic of San Miguel

Serena Black

By Serena Black

For the Lowe family,

For all the years of love and laughter.

Prologue

"Ta-da! What do you think?" Montana said, excited by her purchase.

"You brought a lime tree," Indi said, reading the pot's label.

Her sister's lack of enthusiasm might have been underwhelming, but that still didn't put a dampener on Montana's moment.

"It represents life. James and my life together. Our home, roots, you know," she said.

"The limes being your babies," Indi giggled.

"Maybe," she laughed.

"It's a citrus tree."

"It's a representation, Indi," she sighed.

"But why a lime tree? Why not get a rose bush, you know, easier to grow and pretty to look at?"

"Because a lime tree is also practical. I can use them in my baking, drinks, you know, stuff like that. Besides aren't lime trees supposed to bring luck?"

"I have no idea," Indi shrugged.

Montana was resigned to the fact her sister didn't find the lime tree as exciting as she did. In a way she understood since she was the first of her siblings to not only get engaged but also move out of the family home and into her own place. Therefore everything to Montana was exciting. Making the place she and James called home, the place they were going to start growing their lives together, Montana wanted to stamp their mark on it. It didn't even matter that it was a rental because it was still theirs.

Indi felt a little guilty for teasing her sister and not being more excited for her in her new home. She just missed Montana a lot. They were the closest out of the six Chan siblings because they were not only the two eldest but girls. The next two younger siblings were boys and so Montana and Indiana shared everything.

Although Indi was truly happy Montana had fallen in love with James, she was also a little sad that now they would spend much less time together.

Knowing that life moves on, Indi decided to show her happiness and support of her older sister.

"Well, if a lime tree is supposed to bring you luck, I'm hoping a lemon tree will bring twice the luck," she said, producing the young tree.

Montana's reaction made Indi laugh.

"You just gave me a hard time and you brought me a lemon tree," Montana said, incredulous.

"What a fluke, huh?" she giggled. "I was hoping that you didn't go out and buy yourself one. See you're lucky already."

"Is it one I need to put in the ground?"

"No. It's a miniature so you can pot it and take it with you when you buy your own house, then you can plant it in the ground if you want."

"I love it. Thanks, Indi." Tears were welling up in Montana's eyes. It seemed so silly to cry over a tree but it was what it represented — her sister supporting her relationship, her next step in life. She hugged Indi tight. "I love you and miss you."

"Me too. Its not the same ringing you and the bedroom feels really empty. Although I have to say, its nice to have more space," she chuckled.

The sisters had shared a room most of their lives and for Indi it was weird not to have Montana's presence, knowing her sister wasn't ever coming back, and so she sometimes just felt a sense of loss.

"Well, you can come over anytime," Montana said, wiping her eyes. "Hey, maybe we can have sleepovers."

"Great idea." Indi's face brightened. "Hanging out in our jammies, eating ice cream and gossiping."

"Ooh, and watching chick flicks."

"I love it. Let's do it."

Both women seemed much happier now that they'd found a way to still keep their close bond tight.

After Indi left, Montana wandered around the house torn between being ecstatic at having her own place and space and missing the constant noise of living with her family. Being the eldest of six children, she spent most of her life frustrated and irritated by the lack of privacy from her younger siblings and being like another mother — always around for them to vent or get advice they didn't want to ask their parents for.

Now that she didn't have the constant din, she missed it but there were always family dinners and Indi seemed happy to have a room to herself making the others jealous they were still sharing.

That weekend she and James went shopping for two brightly coloured spacious pots for their new plants and bought all the supplies to tend them. It was quite exciting to do something so grown-up as a couple, to make the decisions together. It didn't matter that it was only for the garden, it still felt great.

A while later she and James stood and stared happily at the end result. Two fully potted miniature citrus trees standing side by side. It was a perfect moment.

"Do you want to be the lemon or lime?" he teased, nuzzling her neck as he embraced her from behind.

"Whichever grows the best," she said, turning to face him.

"Shall we celebrate the potting of our trees?"

"Hmm, I like the sound of that."

Afterwards, Montana cuddled close to James and had to admit enjoying this part of living by themselves. They had privacy whenever they wanted.

In time her citrus trees bloomed with flowers, Montana was giddy with excitement since she hadn't expected it nor so many.

"Look," she squealed. "They're flowering."

James just laughed, happy Montana was happy.

The next time she looked out the window, she noticed that nearly all the flowers had disappeared.

"Where did all the flowers go?" she said, bewildered.

"The wind might have blown them off. It's been pretty gusty lately."

His explanation made sense but still she was disappointed.

James was enjoying his life with Montana and it amused him at how focussed she was on the citrus trees. He watched her talking to them as she watered them and when she caught any birds pecking around in the pot dirt looking for food or taking a bath, she'd scold them as she shooed them away. Those were the times he couldn't help but smile.

The only way life could get any better would be the day he married her in front of all their family and friends.

* * *

How had it gone from being the happiest time in Montana's life to the saddest in the blink of an eye? One minute she was marrying the man she loved and the next, he was gone?

For everyone who gathered it was a sad day, but for some of those mourners it was bleaker than the coldest, wintriest day.

James Dobson was dead.

Gone too soon.

He barely started life before it suddenly and tragically ended.

His young wife and widow, Montana stoically watched her husband's casket being lowered into the ground before bursting into uncontrollable tears. Family comforted her, and as much as she felt their warmth and love, she felt cold.

How was she ever going to live without James by her side? The life they both dreamed of was now gone.

Chapter One

The sunrise on San Miguel was as spectacular as Montana imagined it to be. The fine white pristine sand on the beach began to sparkle and the soothing sound of the gently lapping waves let her mind relax and wander back to happier times in her life with her family and friends and James.

James with his happy-go-lucky personality who could always make her smile and laugh. She and James attended the same high school and although they didn't socialise in the same circles, they still knew of each other as kids do. She was twenty when they ran into each other at a party.

After that, call it coincidence, luck or fate the two of them just seemed to keep running into each other.

One night they were both at a mutual friend's party and although the place was crowded, Montana saw James across the room smiling as he talked to someone. It was his smile that sent her stomach fluttering, and the fact she secretly hoped he would be here.

Now she didn't know how to approach him. Should she just walk up to him to say hi, or perhaps hope he saw her? Maybe she could pretend she didn't know he was here and nonchalantly bump into him once again? Yes, she liked that idea, accidental meeting it was.

"Oh, I'm so sorry," she said, after she took a step back and bumped into someone, knowing it was James.

As he turned, the force of his smile upon recognition of her, made her heart race.

"Well, well, well, fancy seeing you here," he chuckled.

"I could ask if you're stalking me, after all, what are the odds that we meet, yet again?" she flirted.

"Not possible since I was at a friend's birthday and didn't want to leave but since I promised Frankie I'd come and meet his new girlfriend, I couldn't not come. So sorry, your theory is blown out of the water. However, I could say the same thing about you. Perhaps you're stalking me?" he teased.

"Not likely," she laughed. "I'm a last-minute invite because I bumped into Grace this morning at the supermarket.

"So you're friends with Grace and I'm friends with Frankie, sounds like kismet to me," he grinned.

Light-heartedly agreeing they were obviously destined to be together, he took her phone number and asked her out on a date.

After that night, they started dating and were happily married until a year ago. Where the rest of her siblings were starting to have itchy feet, wanting to leave the family nest and explore the world, Montana was happy to stay in New Zealand, marry the love of her life and have a family.

That had been the plan until one tragic day, James came home after a morning run and hadn't felt quite right. After a rest and still not feeling quite a hundred percent she managed to talk him into going to the hospital, but he never came home. He suffered a massive heart attack and nothing could be done to save him.

The shock and devastation of his death turned her into a zombie. She had no idea what was happening and even when it was time to say goodbye to him at his funeral, it all seemed surreal to her. She saw James everywhere and talked to him often in tears of regret for all the things they never got to do together. She was also terribly angry with him for leaving everyone at such a young age, especially her.

Even though her family were a pillar of strength for her, as time went on, even they began to worry more that her grief wasn't subsiding. Montana not only lost her zest for life but became a shell of her former self. The weight of James' death was like a heavy cloak surrounding her that she just couldn't seem to shake off, neither would it lighten so she could keep moving. Her legs were heavy, unable to move forward because each step meant she was one further past his death, and she was torn between the guilt of living and moving on with her life, and standing still in a moment that could never be changed.

Her once bright and happy future disappeared, vanished in a puff of smoke. Sometimes she wanted to believe James was still alive — that everyone was lying to her. Maybe he was in trouble and couldn't tell her or perhaps he was in a Witness Protection Programme because he had seen something to make him a target of someone wanting to kill him.

Deep down Montana knew this was all just her way of trying to cope but the nights were the worst. The endless nights of thinking about James and that fateful day.

She repeatedly went over it a million times in her head, all the *what ifs*. If only she insisted on taking him to the hospital earlier. If only he hadn't gone for his normal routine morning run.

If only…if only…if only.

Those two simple words constantly went round and round in circles over and over and always made her despair that she had missed something, that James' death was somehow her fault.

The month before his death he had a cold, was that a sign he was about to have a heart attack? The silly fights over nothing, having to pay the bills, did the stress of all that take a toll on his health? All these questions drove her insane and everyone in her family said the same thing every time she would mention something — that it had been unforeseen. Even the doctors said the same thing but still, she was sure it was her fault, that she had missed vital signs.

She read up on heart attack warnings so she could now recite the warning signs the medical fraternity advised because there was no way she was ever going to let someone else she loved die because of her ignorance.

Although she couldn't remember the day when she realised life was still ongoing and she wasn't a part of it, it brought relief and delight to her family and friends that Montana was finally ready to rejoin the world again.

Her best friends, Antonia Patterson and Isabella Esteban were ecstatic when Montana decided to rejoin their friendship again in a more interactive way. Before Montana even knew what was happening, her friends suggested a trip overseas to somewhere sunny and hot with beaches to relax, somewhere to get away from it all.

"Come on, Mon. Consider it a change of scenery."

"A fresh start."

"A new chapter."

They both gently coaxed her and as terrified as Montana was that she was somehow betraying James by moving on, it not only seemed like a good idea, but she definitely could use a change of scenery.

While at first Montana may not have been a hundred percent sure about this trip, she could now admit while sitting alone on the beach on San Miguel watching the sunrise, that her best friends were right — this was the balm she needed to help heal her broken heart.

Salty moisture pricked at her eyes and she hoped it was from the spray of the ocean and the sun's glimmer of rays, but she knew they were tears. Tears for James and the life they could have had together. Tears for still missing him so much.

Even though she would always love and miss James, she also knew she needed to move on. However, every now and then flashes of guilt suddenly hit and she would either be in tears or frozen, trying to find the courage to tell herself it was okay, that James would understand and want her to be happy, just as she would have wanted the same for him if the roles were reversed.

Not realising she needed this alone time — this sunrise — as another step in dealing with her grief, she couldn't help but feel a sense of peace.

Looking out onto the horizon, there was a lone surfer who must have decided now was also a great time to be in the water — just him and the ocean. The waves were much bigger further out and it took her a while to even realise there was someone out there. His figure was small in the distance and his black wetsuit blended in with the ocean until the sun rose enough to lighten the sky and the world about her.

Keeping her eye on him and the horizon, when she hadn't seen him for ages, she quickly stood brushing the sand off her bottom, urgently scanning the water for him. Her heart quickened as she became worried something may have happened. Should she go and get help? Suddenly someone appeared and she released a loud breath when she saw him running out of the surf towards her.

Relief flooded through her, glad nothing had happened to him. Smiling to herself at the silliness of her worry over a complete stranger, she plopped back down on the sand amused by the fact there was an entire beach where he could have exited the water, and yet he ended up by her.

Planned or not, the image of him coming out of the surf dripping wet with a broad smile reminded Montana so much of James that for a brief minute she thought she was seeing him. James had the same dark brown hair and amazing smile that lit up his face. As he jogged towards her, she couldn't help smiling back at this handsome wet stranger.

"Morning! Beautiful sunrise, isn't it?" he said.

"Spectacular. How was the water?"

She realised in an instant that although at a distance this man looked like James, close up he was nothing like James at all. His accent for one, sent shivers down her spine, his face more rugged than James' baby face. It could be the fact that the stranger hadn't shaved yet and so the dark bristle made him look older, perhaps if he shaved, he would look more youthful.

"Refreshing, you should have a dip. It's nice to have some alone time since no one is normally up this early around here."

Most of the tourists stayed up late drinking and clubbing in the small town and then slept the mornings away.

"Oh, I'm sorry. I didn't mean to intrude," she said, pink spots forming on her cheeks.

"Don't worry about it. Actually, if I didn't want any company, I wouldn't have left the water."

He lay his board on the sand wanting to make sure she understood that he didn't mind her company, if anything, he was the one intruding on her peace and quiet.

Montana watched him unzip his wetsuit and peel down the top half to reveal a very well-tanned and toned torso and arms. Her reaction to such a sight scared her. Not since James had she even thought of a man sexually. Yes, she ogled men in magazines and fantasised, but it wasn't the same as being so close to a half-naked man…alone…on a beach. Anyone arriving now might think they were lovers and she quickly looked out at the view, her cheeks flushed.

"Mind if I join you?" Not waiting for an answer he sat down beside her.

This was all wrong. She was supposed to be sitting here with her husband, sitting here in the most memorable of romantic moments — the kind of moment that lived on in a couple's life. James was supposed to be on this holiday with her, not her two best friends who were still soundly sleeping.

Montana was also supposed to be yelling or at least firmly telling this stranger in no uncertain terms that he was too arrogant by far to just feel at home to sit beside her and that at any minute now, James would be here to give him a piece of his mind for daring to hit on his wife.

What she wasn't supposed to feel, was comforted and comfortable in the silence next to a complete stranger. Why hadn't she told him to go away or better yet, why hadn't she moved away? Because I was here first, was the first stubborn thought to enter her mind even though she knew it was just a lame excuse for staying where she was and not moving.

Why didn't he speak? She knew he knew English even if it was with a sexy accent. Why didn't he tell her why he felt compelled to sit next to her on a deserted beach? Why did he have to be here in the first place?

She desperately wanted to blame him for ruining such a

beautiful and glorious sunrise, but deep down she couldn't. If anything, she wanted to thank him for his silent company and the quiet strength she felt he was lending or perhaps she was siphoning it from him unawares.

It felt unnerving to be this comfortable with a complete stranger but still, there they sat, side by side in silence looking out at the horizon with the sun now rising up in the sky making the ocean sparkle.

Looking at her watch, she realised she should get back and meet her friends for breakfast depending on if they were awake yet or not. It didn't worry her if they were still asleep, she could use the time to just relax in peace and quiet, much like now but alone. Perhaps she could even get in another chapter of her book.

Standing and wiping sand off her clothes, she looked down at the stranger.

"I have to go. Thanks for the company."

He looked up and smiled making her stomach do a funny flip and raised his hand to wave.

"See you around."

Watching her walk off, Lucas sat there thinking about the woman on the beach. He saw her arrive when he was surfing and it intrigued him. She was the first person he had seen come down to the beach so early. Deciding after a while to wrap up his surfing and meet her, he wasn't disappointed.

Up close she was stunning. Her long black silky hair was tied up in a simple ponytail. She had no make-up on and so at a guess, he put her in her mid to late twenties. The simple, plain white v-neck tee shirt and khaki green capri pants showed off her slender figure when she stood, but it was her brown eyes and incredible smile that got his attention. He knew she liked what she saw when he unzipped his wetsuit. Most women did but when he caught a glance at her pink tongue which flicked out quickly to moisten her lips, there was a strong reaction in his gut.

Probably what surprised him the most wasn't her cute accent which also did strange things to his insides, but that they sat in a comfortable silence just watching the water and the sun finish rising, with her never making any effort to engage him in conversation. That had to be a first for him, meeting a female not trying to hit on him or just talking because they didn't like the silence. This woman was the complete opposite of any he had ever known.

Having been in San Miguel with his cousins for three days already, he hadn't seen her before now. Had she just arrived? Was she here alone or with friends? Then the thought she was here on a romantic holiday created an unusual sensation in his stomach as was the thought he was being silly hoping he would run into her again?

San Miguel wasn't the biggest of islands and the town itself was quite small and quaint. Still the urge to accidentally run into her again and get to know her was appealing. The waves were still large and so he stood, zipped himself back up and went back into the water, leaving all thought behind him.

Chapter Two

Montana returned to the room to find her friends now awake yet still in bed.

"Hey, we've been wondering where you got to?" Toni said.

"I just went to watch the sunrise on the beach," she said, not mentioning her encounter with a handsome and mysterious stranger.

The three women in the room were best friends since high school with Antonia and Montana having known each other since they were children and Isabella only joining them when her family moved from Spain to New Zealand for her father's work.

Antonia and Montana won over Isabella with their friendliness and sense of humour as they liked to tease Isabella for her 'big city European ways' and her exotic

Spanish looks attracting all the boys, saying that was the only reason they wanted to be friends with her.

They also took to calling her Izzy, which in the beginning she hated, thinking it was a trashy sounding nickname. Everyone she knew called her Bella for short, but Montana and Antonia wouldn't let up and after she had a couple of scatterbrain moments — in which they couldn't help but tease and call her Dizzy Izzy — Izzy knew she was never going to get rid of the awful nickname.

Over time, she enjoyed being called Izzy as she came to view it as acceptance of their close friendship. As soon as she embraced the nickname, she realised her friends weren't being mean and trying to make her feel bad, on the contrary, they were actually trying to make her feel included so Isabella learned to love the nickname as long as only her best friends used it and no one else.

Both friends swore the nickname made Izzy more Kiwi, whether it was the truth or they were lying, she never did find out, but she did miss being called Izzy. Back in Spain, people thought she was crazy when she mentioned her nickname. Why on earth would someone as beautiful as Bella want to be called Izzy and that was when Izzy realised her friends were right. Her crazy adventurous 'Kiwi' side was Izzy, her more demure classy Spanish side was Bella.

These days, Izzy lived in Spain and it had been a while since the three friends had all seen each other, making this was the perfect holiday to reconnect.

Seeing Izzy at the airport in Miami before they caught the next plane to San Miguel, made them all squeal and shriek like teenagers before constantly talking from the time they met up until they finally went to bed later that night.

Montana felt like her old self once she was back in the company of her best friends which made her more relaxed and at ease. This morning was the first time she thought of James since her holiday started and part of her felt a little guilty about it.

"So girls, what shall we do after this?" Toni said, as they enjoyed their brunch sitting under an umbrella in the sun.

"I don't know about you two but I wouldn't mind working on my tan and checking out if there are any *hot* guys to perve on," Izzy said, making them all giggle since she had naturally olive skin so her tan didn't need any more work.

"I agree. I refuse to go home pasty white. I want everyone to know I've not only been on holiday but to somewhere hot and sunny, and to also make them jealous of my tan," Toni laughed. "Being able to ogle hot guys is just a bonus."

Montana was just happy to go with the flow, although secretly wondered if she would see her mystery stranger again at the beach. The thought made her smile to herself yet she refused to get her hopes up and besides, she wasn't here to find a man, just to have a good time with her friends.

They went back to the room to change into their bikinis and apply sunscreen, before packing their bags and heading to the beach.

The beach was now sprinkled with people lying everywhere sunbathing, compared to the desert it was earlier this morning. The girls found themselves a spot out of the way and while Toni and Izzy were happy to lie there and sunbathe, Montana however, wanted a swim. The water was just as refreshing as her stranger had said and she didn't hesitate to wade in up to her waist before diving under, not caring if her hair got wet.

After paddling around for a while before getting out and flicking water on her friends who squealed and moaned while she laughed, she grabbed her book and hat, lay down on her stomach and began to read and dry off.

The sight of two extremely sexy guys coming out of the water caused a stir and Izzy and Toni were now propped up on their elbows staring like every other female on the beach, especially when the two men unzipped their wetsuits to show off their well-toned torsos.

"Mon, you have to see these gorgeous hunks," Izzy said.

"Yes, oh so gorgeous," Toni sighed.

Turning around to have a look, her heart started racing wondering if one of the men was the stranger she met just this morning. Disappointment shot through her when she saw he wasn't, making her shake her head at how silly she was being.

However, she was amused to see two women walking towards the men obviously to chat them up judging by the appreciative eyeing of the men's bodies however, the two men seemed oblivious to the approaching women and were instead looking over in their direction.

Watching the men politely chat to the women, whose faces deflated as the conversation progressed, it wasn't until after the ladies left looking disappointed, the two men then approached them grinning from ear to ear.

"Ladies."

One of the men spoke with a rather delightful sounding accent Montana couldn't quite pick, but she thought it sounded very similar to her sunrise companion.

Stop it! she chided herself feeling foolish to keep having runaway thoughts about her mystery stranger.

"Enjoying the sunshine?" the man said, his eyes never leaving Toni as he sat down by her feet before anyone could tell him that they weren't interested.

While the girls' sunglasses hid the fact they had also been discreetly ogling the men, Toni was now blushing.

"Yes, we are, thanks," Izzy said.

Montana could feel the electricity crackle between the four people and decided as she was indeed the odd person out, to politely excuse herself to go for another swim giving them some time alone to get to know each other.

Lucas was having a little break from the stresses of work with his best friends and cousins, Marco and Antonio, and they decided to holiday on San Miguel because of the great surfing.

At breakfast, his cousins could only stare out at the water and Lucas knew they were keen for a surf since the waves were looking good.

"We're off for a surf."

"Coming?"

"You go ahead. I've already been in this morning so I'll join you later."

His cousins didn't waste another minute and left the table leaving him in peace and quiet. Sighing, he picked up the phone and called his father who wanted him to check in

An hour later, he finally hung up. It wasn't that he didn't enjoy talking to his father, but sometimes Franco Romero did tend to ramble on about nothing and as politely as Lucas could, he reminded his father that he was on holiday and was relieved when his father took the hint and said goodbye. From his hotel room he could still see the surf was good so he grabbed his board and went in search of his cousins.

Lucas scanned the beach and water looking for Antonio and Marco while he walked along, when he finally saw them chatting to some girls. Typical, he shook his head smiling to himself, they were never ones to pass up an opportunity to meet a pretty girl and jogged along to join them. Just as he approached, he saw a vision in a black string bikini emerge from the water and walk straight towards the group. He couldn't see her face properly as her arm blocked it as she pushed her hair back, but her curvy body made his instantly react. He also admired her cute little derriere as she bent over to squeeze water out of her hair.

"Luc!" Tonio said, waving him over. "Come and meet some lovely ladies, we've just met."

"This is Toni, Izzy and…" Marco paused not knowing the third girl's name.

She flashed Marco a smile.

"Monta…" She turned and looked straight into the face of her handsome stranger. "Na."

Everything seemed to freeze all around her before she blinked and Marco interrupted the moment.

"We're Marco, Tonio and Lucas."

"Nice to meet you all," she said, having to tear her eyes off the man called Lucas.

Her two friends didn't miss a beat.

"Do you two know each other?" Toni said, grabbing everyone's interest.

"Actually, we met this morning on the beach. I had gone for a surf and —"

"I went to watch the sunrise," she quickly said, as they both stared and grinned at each other like they were they only two people in the world.

"Uh-huh," Izzy murmured, exchanging a look with Toni.

"Well since we now all know each other, how about we meet up for dinner?" Tonio said, and the girls readily agreed.

Montana said nothing and just sat back down on her towel and went to put her sunglasses and hat back on so she didn't have to look at Lucas.

"Let me get that for you."

Lucas' husky voice was right by her ear sending shivers down her spine as he took the sunscreen from her. His gentle touch and the coolness of the lotion had her at boiling point as he rubbed it all over her back. There was something so intimate at letting another person touch you in broad daylight so sensually. The last man to put sunscreen on her was James.

Panic immediately flared inside her and she quickly grabbed her things and stuffed them into her bag.

"I have to go," she said, quickly standing and then briskly walking away leaving everyone slightly stunned.

She was wiping the tears from her eyes when Toni and Izzy caught up with her and put their arms around her.

"Are you okay?" Toni said, concerned.

"Yes, I'm sorry to ruin your day. You should go back and enjoy yourselves."

"Mon, you're our friend. We're here to be with you. Those guys will survive," Izzy said, knowing that right now there would be a bevy of women already flocking around and flirting with them. Silently she hoped their dinner invitation still stood since she found Marco to be her type of guy and wouldn't mind getting to know him a lot better.

They were sitting at the outdoor hotel bar waiting for their drinks in silence.

"So what happened?" Toni said, once their drinks were delivered.

"I don't know. I was enjoying myself until Lucas put sunscreen on me and then I totally freaked. James was the last guy to ever touch me like that," she tearily said, feeling stupid, as both her friends gave her hugs of sympathy.

"It's okay, Mon. It's not your fault. There's always going to be things you have to overcome where James was the last time that happened to you, it's only natural," Toni said.

"Yes, and no one said that you can't feel sad about it," Izzy said.

"I know but I feel so guilty. You know I've only thought of James twice and that's because of Lucas. Is that horrible?" Once again tears welled up in her eyes as her friends replied with an emphatic "no" before giving her a gentle squeeze for support.

"It's okay to move on. It doesn't mean you no longer love James or will forget him — it's more that if you don't live, then you're missing out on your own life. No one knew he was going to have a heart attack. Do you think that he'd want you to sit around moping for him, forever?" Toni said, as gently as possible.

Both Izzy and Toni were devastated for Montana when James died and seeing their best friend have her life turned upside down, both friends felt a sense of helplessness knowing there wasn't anything they could do to really help. Izzy, felt it more so, since she was now back living in Spain. That's why this holiday was so important to the three of them. They wanted Montana to know that they would always be there to support each other.

Toni always thought Montana was so brave, that even when she was in shock and mourning, she didn't totally lose it. Sure, Toni saw Montana's depressed days, especially in the beginning where she questioned every little detail of every little thing in the hope that if only she could find an answer to why James died then she could understand it all better, but there never was an answer. Now seeing her friend so much more like her old self, it was easy to forget what Montana had been through, which it made it much harder when she had sad moments because Montana was like a wounded puppy and Toni and Izzy didn't want their best friend to hurt.

"And if you had known that James was going to die so young, would you still have gone out with him and got married?" Izzy said.

Her two friends made rational sense, yet it was still hard to wrap her head around the fact she not only had another man's hands on her body, but that he made her stomach flutter.

"Do you want to cancel dinner with the boys? We can hang out and do something else if you like," Toni said, but Montana couldn't ruin their holiday romances because of her guilty conscience.

"Don't be silly. Miss a chance to have dinner with three sinful and gorgeous guys with sexy accents," she said, hoping to sound enthusiastic and judging by the bright smiles on her friend's faces, she made the right decision.

"We should go shopping and find ourselves new outfits," Izzy said, making her friends laugh — Izzy used any excuse to shop.

"Great idea," Toni said, and Montana was happy to be swept up in her friends' enthusiasm grateful for the distraction.

They did a bit of browsing around the shops and all found new outfits. Toni bought a gypsy style dress that was a beautiful mix of blues. Izzy found an emerald green mini skirt that had ruffled layers and showed off her long slender legs and a white crocheted singlet top, while Montana found a long gypsy style skirt in a pretty red and a matching peasant blouse in white.

Deciding they'd wear their new outfits to dinner that night, they all giggled at getting ready, which was a feat in itself when there were three women and only one bathroom.

Since Toni *always* took the longest to get ready, they let her go first hoping she'd then hurry a little faster. Izzy went next and then Montana but as it turned out, they were all constantly in and out of the bathroom forgetting things anyway, yet it still worked because soon they were all ready to leave.

Chapter Three

Although Montana had no idea where the restaurant was because she was swimming when the others discussed it, none of that mattered because now she was supposed to see these men again after running away from them at the beach, and therefore her nerves were swirling with anxiousness.

What would their dates make of that? Would they be feeling sorry for Lucas for being paired up with the weird one? Toni, seeing her face gave her hand a quick squeeze and she returned a small smile.

"Do you think they'll be there, and waiting for us?" Toni was jiggling with nerves and excitement.

"I hope so but who knows? They may have found other women and ditched us," Izzy said, trying hard not to seem disappointed by the prospect.

"I know it's silly considering we just met, but I truly felt like Tonio and I had a connection," Toni said, now anxious.

"I'm so sorry. If I hadn't freaked out then you wouldn't be so worried," Montana said.

"It's not your fault, Mon. Besides, if they don't turn up then you've just saved us from a bunch of sleaze bags who only wanted sex," Izzy said. "With or without them, we'll have a great night out as we always do."

"Izzy's right, Mon. It's not your fault and now we'll get to see what their true intentions are," Toni said.

Montana remained silent unable to decide whether she wanted to have saved her friends from some holiday Romeos or if she wanted to see her mystery stranger again.

"I sort of hope they do turn up especially since Marco is super cute," Izzy said.

"So is Tonio. Isn't it funny that we practically have the same name?"

"Its fate," Izzy sighed.

"I hope so."

Hearing the wistful longing in her best friends' voices reassured Montana that she made the right decision to come to this dinner. If anyone deserved a great holiday romance it was Toni for whom dating didn't come easy. On the other hand, Izzy was the complete opposite; men were like bees to a honey pot.

Being able to give both her friends a chance for a little holiday excitement was Montana's way of showing her appreciation for all their unwavering support.

"What nationality do you think they are?" Toni said.

"Their names sound Italian but who knows, maybe they're fiery Spanish," Montana teased.

"No, they're definitely Italian," Izzy said.

"Either is romantic," Toni sighed.

Both Izzy and Montana tried hard not to laugh but it slipped out, not that Toni cared in the slightest. She was still daydreaming of the handsome young man from the beach.

The taxi stopped halfway up the mountain and as they got out, the view took all their breaths away. It was spectacular with the restaurant overlooking the town and the ocean.

As they reached the front entrance three men who were all dressed similarly in trousers and open neck shirts appeared out of nowhere complimenting them and offering each of them a flower.

"Ciao Bellas, we're so glad you made it. You all look bellissima, beautiful," Marco said, unable to take his eyes off Izzy.

"Well, that answers that question," Montana said, under her breath.

Izzy nudged her trying to stifle a giggle as Toni looked entranced by Tonio who only had eyes for her as well.

Was Montana imagining things or did the three men look relieved they had shown up? Guilt flickered within her again, imagining what the men must have thought while waiting to see if they would turn up or not, since she ran off and left her friends chasing after her.

"Thank you," she mumbled, as she took the flower Lucas offered her, but was unable to look at him.

Going to follow the others inside, Lucas' hand grabbed her slender wrist and tugged her so she stopped to look at him. Her heart was once again zooming at his touch and nearness.

"Did I do something to upset you this afternoon?" he said, his voice low and concerned.

"Don't be silly," she teased. "Why would you think that?"

"Because you ran away like you were on fire."

"It wasn't you," she said, feeling guilty. "It was one of those moments, you know like you think you've forgotten to turn the oven off. No big deal."

Although Montana was trying to brush off what happened, he could see in her eyes there was something that she was hiding and didn't pursue it any further.

"Here, allow me," he said, taking the flower from her hand and tucking it behind her ear. "There, that looks better."

His eyes flared and for an instant she felt a moment of panic thinking he was going to kiss her. Blinking, she quickly turned and went to find their table, needing to put a little breathing space between them.

Lucas frowned as he struggled with Montana's nervousness. She hadn't been at all like this when they first met this morning on the beach at sunrise and he had no idea what was making her so jumpy around him now. He could only think she felt the same electricity that passed through him every time he saw her and was afraid of it.

Never being one to pressure a woman into anything, if anything he never needed to, but in this instance, he wasn't sure even his persuasive charm was going to get him far either. Still deep in thought over Montana's skittishness, he headed to the table to join the rest of the group.

As the wine and laughter flowed over stories being traded while getting to know each other, Lucas was aware Montana held herself back. The stories of the three of them from school she was happy to join in but anything else, she was quiet.

"You okay?" he said so only she could hear, and she nodded without even looking at him making him even more frustrated since she hadn't looked at him all night. It was like having a giant wall between them and he didn't like it at all. He wanted to break it down and have that flirty banter and teasing his cousins were having, along with the looks of desire and promise of what the night held.

Montana never felt as aware of a man as she was with Lucas sitting next to her all night at dinner. The occasional accidental brush with their arms or the bang of their knees was driving her crazy. She couldn't look at him because if she did, she knew she'd probably do something really stupid like want to madly flirt with him or stare into his eyes.

The others proved enough of a distraction so she didn't have to join in the conversation as much, but even then all good things had to end and by the time they were having coffee, the air was crackling between all the couples, except her and Lucas.

The ladies did the time-honoured tradition of going to the restroom together while the men paid the bill. While they were in there, they discussed their plans since sharing a room wasn't conducive to ending a romantic evening by any stretch of the imagination. Montana was happy to get another room for the night if they just gave her time to grab some stuff since she wasn't planning on sleeping with Lucas. That left Izzy and Toni to sort out the room and Toni won out but by the time they emerged and went to find their dates, it turned out that Antonio and Marco had already sorted it and Montana was allowed the room after all, but had to let Lucas share since they were kicking him out.

It was actually a little white lie the men cooked up since they all had their own rooms at their hotel and because Lucas needed an excuse to spend time with Montana without scaring her off, his cousins readily agreed to the lie.

Three taxis were ordered to give each couple privacy and Lucas asked Montana if she wanted to go somewhere else hoping it would make her more relaxed in his company.

"Would you like to do something else? Clubbing? A bar, perhaps?" he said, helping her into the taxi.

"Do you mind if we just went back to the hotel and went for a walk on the beach?"

Her anxiety kicked up a notch knowing she definitely didn't want to be locked in a room with him. It would be too close and confining for her comfort and peace of mind.

"Sure, that's a great idea," he said, relieved she didn't want to do anything else.

They rode in silence and neither spoke until they got to the beach. Montana took off her shoes and went to loop her arm around his before she caught herself and clasped her hands behind her back. Lucas shoved his hands into his pockets not trusting himself not to touch her.

As there was only half a moon for light, he couldn't see her face properly.

"Your friends seem really nice," he said.

"They are the best friends in the entire world." She whole-heartedly agreed. "We used to hang out at my place a lot since they don't have siblings and I have a truckload. I think that they may have at one stage had crushes on my brothers which you know, grossed me out."

His chuckle in the darkness made her stomach do somersaults.

"I know what you mean, although it was me who had a crush on one of my sister's friends. I thought she was so hot and pretty much panted after her, making my sister mad when I kept hanging around being annoying. Then when I realised just how high maintenance she was, I was so glad she wouldn't give me the time of day."

"How many siblings do you have?" she said, curious. It sounded like he was close to them or at least had a loving relationship with them.

"Three sisters. How about you?"

"Three sisters and two brothers."

They continued to walk in silence with Montana feeling more comfortable being with Lucas under the cover of darkness before Lucas asked if she wanted to turn around and head back. Agreeing, they turned but she fell off balance and he caught her. He could hear the slight hitch in her breathing and before he could stop himself, he lowered his head and kissed her.

Montana knew being held in Lucas' arms should have her screaming and running away in fright, but it felt so right. Maybe it was because it was so dark and she couldn't see him properly, but she knew that was a lie. Her own heart was loudly pounding so she couldn't even hear the ocean anymore and then when his mouth found hers all she could do was melt into him.

He kissed with such finesse that in no time she was opening her mouth to him, welcoming his conquest. Her breasts tightened in response and her stomach swirled with an aching need she hadn't felt in a long time.

They stood and kissed for ages with neither making a move for anything more. When he finally pulled apart, his breathing was just as ragged as hers making her feel better it was a two way street, this funny feeling.

Putting his arm around her shoulders and hers around his waist, she leaned her head on his shoulder and he relaxed at the intimate gesture as they walked in silence stopping every few metres or so to kiss some more that by the time they were back at the start, Montana felt a stab of disappointment.

"I think I'd better make sure that you understand that I'm not going to be sleeping with you tonight. I hope you don't think I'm a tease," she said, grateful for the darkness to hide her embarrassment as guilt once again washed over her. How could she have forgotten James after a short stroll? Because of Lucas' sensationally, mind-blowing, forget-everything-including-your-name kisses, she thought.

He wrapped his arms around her and kissed her again before responding.

"It's fine. I'm happy to use one of the other beds provided I get a cold shower first," he teased, his forehead was touching hers as she gave a small smile of relief that he wasn't going to pressure her.

Lucas had no idea what was stopping him from persuading Montana into his bed because he knew if her kisses were anything to go by, he could do it but there was obviously something holding her back judging by the way she anxiously told him they were sleeping in separate beds.

At least the wall was gone and he was grateful for that.

Chapter Four

By the time they got back to the room Montana was a basket of nerves, her brain ready to explode from all the knots she'd tangled herself into. She shouldn't have led Lucas on by kissing him, but the moonlight and darkness obviously made her mind think James was the man walking beside her, not Lucas.

She nibbled on her bottom lip knowing she just told herself a lie, but forgetting James so easily wasn't something she could accept and that was the problem.

"Feel free to use the bathroom first, I'll just tidy up," she said, her eyes darting around to see what exactly needed to be tidied. Luckily, they hadn't strewn clothes everywhere so the room looked like a tornado had hit.

"Sure, thanks," he said, going into the bathroom and chuckling at all the toiletries everywhere.

He stood there for a moment looking into the mirror trying to understand what was it about Montana that had him all out of sorts, making him do and agree to things he wouldn't normally do for any woman. Most of the women he knew liked to play coy and have him 'persuade' them into having sex, it was all part of the foreplay. If a woman didn't want sex, he was okay with that and would leave and although he could make up an excuse and do just that, tonight he didn't want to. He wanted to spend as much time with Montana as possible — sex or not. There was just something about her that called to him. Something he had never experienced before and therefore wanted to try and see if he could work out what it was about Montana that made him feel like this.

Knowing his cousins were right this minute doing bedroom gymnastics while he wasn't even close irked him in a small way as well.

At the restaurant when he told Marco and Tonio that Montana seemed to blow hot and cold with him — and them being the loving cousins they were — they just laughed at his misfortune and wished him luck. Then he slyly came up with the idea of pretending to need a place to sleep and it worked. Those kisses she gave him were full of latent desire, he just needed to find a way to break through the invisible shell surrounding her because he knew that once he did, she'd be all molten lava ready to erupt.

Montana was relieved she didn't sleep in sexy lingerie but wore one of James' oversized tee shirts however, now she had changed, a part of her felt a little embarrassed by it.

There was also a tiny flicker of desire which wanted to share a bed with Lucas.

But how did you tell someone to whom you just clearly spelt out you weren't going to sleep with them, that you now did want to sleep with them, just not in a sexual way but rather in a comforting way. It had been a long time since she slept in a man's arms and she missed that feeling of security and love.

The only trouble was her attraction to Lucas. She couldn't deny it existed and knew that if she spent the night in the same bed, she would want more. He already wanted more, however, she was too scared to give herself to anyone that intimately.

James had been her first and only lover, yet she didn't remember his touch ever making her feel so many different things all at the same time or muddle her brain so she was a puddle of mush, like Lucas did.

Shaking her head telling herself it was just because she was on holiday, in a different place far from home that she wasn't acting or thinking like herself. No, she'd stick firmly to her original decision — separate beds — it was safer all round.

When he came out, she was busy tidying and looking up, her mouth went instantly dry. His shirt was undone so a strip of toned tanned chest was showing and everything in her started going haywire. This was worse than seeing him half naked at the beach because this was in the intimacy of a hotel room.

"I have a souvenir tee shirt that you could use," she said, nonchalant.

"Thanks, but I don't…" The words *sleep in anything* hung in the air. "I'll be okay," he quickly said.

"Oh, okay," she mumbled, feeling stupid. Of course a man like him didn't wear pyjamas, he didn't need to. He probably had a different woman warming his bed every night making pyjamas superfluous.

On shaky legs she went to brush her teeth, her breathing once again slightly ragged, her heart racing. She needed to stop drooling over him.

When she came out, she exhaled a breath of relief seeing him already in bed as she hopped into hers and turned off the light.

They both lay awake in the dark listening to each other's breathing. Lucas couldn't believe that seeing a woman in an oversize tee shirt could be such a turn on. He was more used to blatantly obvious sleepwear that showed a woman's body not hid it but on Montana, it just added to her sexiness.

He spoke into the darkness.

"Tell me about growing up in New Zealand?"

"What can I say? Being part of a large family and even larger extended family makes me pretty much related to at least half of the local Chinese community through various marriages," she joked. "Being the eldest of six children, let's just say there were constant arguments, yelling, teasing and laughing over the years. Oh, and let's not forget the door slamming, which was probably more us girls being overly dramatic all the time. I don't think my brothers ever slammed a door."

Lucas smiled. It seemed his own sisters were much the same growing up.

"Being the eldest also meant I was *constantly* babysitting or looking after the others, which was such a pain when all your friends were going out or even just hanging out. I'd have to either bring my siblings with me, or not go, or if I was lucky, friends would be willing to hang out at my house. Fortunately, a lot of my friends understood and were willing to have my siblings tag along and join in."

Montana always thought the order of their births made it a lot easier when it came to getting along — two girls, two boys and then two girls. While they were a close-knit family, each sibling also had their own same sex sibling they were closest to.

She was surprised Lucas hadn't asked the question everyone she met always did — how did she get her unusual name? Even people she met briefly always asked. Did this mean Lucas was that one in a million person who just didn't find her name unusual or rare, or perhaps he just wasn't that interested in her except possibly sexually. Her mind denied that was the truth, after all, hadn't he just asked about her childhood?

Ever since they were little, everyone the Chan siblings met found their names amusing. During their childhood, they all hated it but now that they were older, they found it a good laugh and sometimes it even turned into a party trick.

Her parents, Thomas and Ivy Chan holidayed in America before they started a family and created such great memories, they decided to name all their children after places in America.

She and Indiana were the two eldest, then came her younger brothers, Boston and Phoenix before her two little sisters, Alexandria and Savannah.

Of course she and Indi loved to tease and lord it over their younger siblings that they were much more important in the family hierarchy since they were named after States and not cities or towns.

This in turn made the boys argue they were at least named after State capitals, which they would all then tease their two baby sisters that they were only named after small cities.

Alexandria and Savannah hated the way their elder sisters bossed them around and used the whole 'State' logic as a reason to make them do something, so to get their own back, they'd tease Montana and Indi by telling them that although they hadn't been named after States, they got the prettier names since they were the prettiest girls in the family.

"Another thing about living with so many siblings is the fact that there is no such thing as privacy at all," she moaned as he smiled — he could imagine.

He heard plenty of his sisters' arguments over sharing a bathroom but luckily being the only boy he got his own space that his sisters still didn't hesitate to invade complaining about why should he get his own space when they had to share, that it wasn't fair.

Montana and Indi shared a room and even though everyone else was told that it was off-limits to them, they constantly found their younger sisters in their room rummaging through their things, trying on their clothes or make-up much to their constant irritation which ended up with yet another round of yelling, screaming and door slamming.

It was worse when Alexandria or Savannah found something embarrassing and then told the rest of the family. Much like the time they found their older sisters' feminine hygiene products and then went around showing everyone or the time when they tried on their bras over the top of their clothes and pranced around the house.

Their mother scolded them but the humiliation occurred and no amount of parental scolding could ever take that moment back, especially when the boys kept making endless teasing younger brother comments to them and to any friends or boyfriends that came over.

Lucas could listen to Montana's voice for hours and noted that apart from this morning, she was only relaxed with him in the darkness when she couldn't see him. Was it something about him that turned her off? That thought didn't sit well with him at all. Still he felt that sense of comfort between them and it made him smile.

"Tell me about your family?" she said.

He, too, also grew up in a close-knit family and where she was from a middle-class family, his was wealthy, but he didn't say.

"Like you my family is very close. In fact, Marco and Tonio aren't just my cousins and best friends but we're more like brothers and we do everything together. We got up to a lot of mischief growing up and we rarely fight, but that's probably because we don't live together and so we each have our own space."

Somewhere during his talking she fell asleep, he could hear it in her steady breathing and he closed his eyes.

Montana was dreaming of James, the first time they met. Then it was their awkward first kiss they shared that made her giggle, and then their clumsy first attempt at sex. It had been a disaster but they managed to laugh about it and it definitely got better after that. The day they moved in together and their dreams for the future were all featured in her dream.

Then for some unknown reason, James kept offering her pasta to eat. It was so random and weird, but she laughed at every plate he brought to her — spaghetti, lasagne, ravioli, and cannelloni. Even though she was so full, he would keep bringing her more and telling her to eat up before he gave her a kiss.

"You know I will always love you and want you to be happy, Mon. Live the life you deserve."

"Don't leave me again. Please, don't go. I miss you so much. I love you."

"I know, I will always love you too. Be happy, Mon." He smiled before disappearing, leaving her bereft.

Lucas woke to Montana's moaning and mumbling. She kept restlessly moving and was becoming more and more agitated. Against his better instincts which told him he shouldn't, he got out of his bed, climbed into hers and held her close to him. She seemed to instantly calm down and went back into a deep sleep as she snuggled into him.

When she woke, she instantly knew something was different. She felt cocooned in strong warmth like she hadn't felt in a long time — that safe and secure feeling — but when she tried to move, she became aware she was encased in strong arms. Panic flared through her.

Lucas was in bed with her!

She didn't remember him getting into the bed and she quickly tried to get away but he held her tightly to him so she was stuck.

Trying to roll out of his arms didn't work so she attempted to move one of them, but all that did was make his arm move down to her hip and then he started caressing her thigh. His hand started to go up and under her tee shirt and she felt the panic return but at least she found a way to escape and took it. Sliding out of the bed and warily standing away from him, while looking at him still asleep.

Was he one of those men who could seduce a woman in his sleep? She almost laughed out loud to herself, of course he was. Hadn't he just started to prove it? She sat on the other bed just watching him. He looked like an angel, the strong silent kind that drew women like moths to a flame.

Remembering her dream about James, she wondered why now. She hadn't had a dream like that before and it scared her. Was she losing James? She couldn't let herself like Lucas too much because then James would be gone and she'd be alone with her guilt.

Quickly dressing, she went for a walk along the beach to clear her thoughts. All it did was make her mind go round and round until she gave herself a headache. Going back to the hotel, she was still none the wiser about anything.

Chapter Five

Lucas woke up and found himself alone in the room. He knew he hadn't been dreaming when he held Montana in his arms last night and could still feel her presence in the bed. He and his cousins were due to leave tonight but he couldn't bring himself to say goodbye, at least not before solving the mystery that was Montana. Maybe Tonio and Marco would also be agreeable to stay for an extra night or two as well.

He was still in bed with his hands behind his head looking at the ceiling when she returned with coffee.

"Morning, coffee?"

Her chipper greeting couldn't hide the fact that Montana was acting as if she didn't know he slept in the same bed as her even though he was still lying in it. Still he sat up and gratefully took the cup from her hand.

"Thanks, sleep well?" he said, as she nodded. They were back to being polite and civil to each other once again.

"When do you have to leave this island paradise?" He was trying to fill the silence.

"Tomorrow afternoon, I think."

"Want to get some breakfast or see what the others are up to?"

"Sure."

He got dressed and just as he went to call his cousins, the room door burst open and a frantic and upset Izzy came rushing in followed by Marco.

"What's wrong?" Montana said, shocked to see them and instantly worried for her friend.

"I have to go home. Now. My parents are really upset," Izzy said, rushing around like a headless chicken, crying and wiping her eyes.

"Why don't you guys wait outside and I'll help Izzy pack," she said.

As soon as the door shut behind them, Izzy immediately crumpled on the bed.

"What's happened?" she said, holding her friend tight as she cried.

"My mum rang to say I needed to get home on the next plane. My abuela's in the hospital," Izzy sobbed. "I hope she's okay."

"Do you want me to come with you?" She wanted to be as supportive as Izzy had been to her.

Sniffing into a tissue, Izzy gave her a small smile.

"Thanks for the offer, but Marco offered to come and Toni, since you know, she's currently in-between jobs."

Wow, that was quick. Marco offering to go with Izzy made Montana happy that their connection was not only mutual but genuine.

"As long as you have support, although I feel bad since you've been there for me and I can't return the favour," she said.

"Don't feel guilty, Mon. I know you'll stay in touch and besides I'm just upset because I'm a million miles away, that's all."

They hugged each other tightly before Toni came bursting into the room.

"What have I missed?" she said, breathless.

The two girls looked at their friend all dishevelled and laughed.

"Looks like someone had a good night," Montana teased, as Toni blushed.

"Or was it a good morning?" Izzy winked, sending them all into giggles and for a brief moment thoughts of Izzy's sick grandmother vanished.

There was a knock at the door and Marco appeared.

"Ladies, I hate to interrupt but the plane leaves in three hours, so do you want to have brunch first?"

"Yes!" The three women said with a resounding shout.

"Great. You pack and us boys will be down in the restaurant waiting for you."

Toni and Izzy rushed around changing and packing while snippets of their night were exchanged. They both felt they had fallen in love after one night making Montana delighted for them.

"Tonio's wonderful," Toni sighed. "Best night of my life."

"That's great. Normally I'd be putting on my motherly hat worrying that you've fallen too fast, but since the three men are cousins, I think it reassures me more," Montana said.

"Are you okay, if I go with Izzy?" Toni said, anxious while Izzy was trying to pack.

"Of course not. She needs you more than me. You're a good friend and it probably doesn't hurt if Marco *and* Antonio are going with you. He must be really spectacular in the sack," she teased, watching her friend's face go beet red.

The room seemed empty without the presence of her friends as they took their suitcases downstairs to meet the boys for brunch. When it was time to leave, Montana cried, sad to say goodbye to her friends while hoping everything was okay with Izzy's grandmother.

"You guys take the plane, I'll fly back commercial," Lucas said.

His cousins looked at him in surprise.

"Aren't you coming with us?" Tonio said.

He gave a quick glance at Montana and saw the brave face she was putting on.

"No, I'll stay and keep Montana company."

"You don't have to do that, its only another night before I leave," she said.

"No, I think we'd all feel better if I stay."

Seeing the sadness in her eyes, he knew no gentleman would leave a lady alone in distress. Everyone nodded their agreement and Montana could only sigh her acceptance, silently grateful he was staying behind with her.

Waving them off, she wiped the tears from her eyes and surprisingly to Lucas, she let him put his arms around her for comfort.

"Hey, want to hit the beach? I could use a surf." He hoped to take her mind off her friends' departure.

"Sure. Why don't I meet you down there in an hour, where we sat yesterday."

"Great. If I'm not there, I might already be in the water. See you soon."

Before she could stop him, he quickly brushed her lips with his and walked away. Watching his retreating back, she now felt all alone.

Montana stood looking at herself in the bathroom mirror. This morning she made up her mind to stay well away from Lucas and not let her memories of James die.

Now everything seemed to have changed in a blink of an eye — her friends' sudden departure and the fact she was here on beautiful San Miguel for one more night, alone with Lucas before she never saw him again. Maybe she could use him as practise for when she went back home, this way she wouldn't freak out if she ever dated again. She was also grateful no one else would be around to know what she was doing, because even she knew her best friends would probably be in two minds over whether or not to support the idea.

By using Lucas as her test date — in hope that she wouldn't flinch or be anxious by another man's touch — if it worked out, perhaps he wouldn't also mind being her holiday one night fling so she could get that nervous and awkward first time after James over and done with. Would he agree to something so…bizarre? Perhaps it was better if she didn't mention it especially since she couldn't exactly say, "Do you mind letting me practise on you to help me get over my dead husband?"

They didn't know each other well enough to be confiding such personal matters. Maybe she could just play the coy, didn't hardly date woman, who wasn't confident with a man since that was the closest to the truth than anything else she could think of.

She changed into an emerald green bikini, grabbed her bag and went to the beach sitting in the same spot where they originally met. It seemed strange to think she only met Lucas yesterday because she felt like she had known him for years.

Looking out at the ocean, there were a few surfers and it took Montana a while to recognise Lucas as one of them out there enjoying himself.

Deciding she needed to go for a swim, she stood and removed her linen cover up, tied up her hair into a ponytail and walked into the water. She splashed around for a while before releasing her hair and squeezing out the excess water as she walked out of the surf. She didn't even notice that a pair of dark brown chocolate eyes were watching her, glittering with desire.

Lucas saw Montana strip to go into the ocean and almost fell off his board. She was wearing a green bikini that seemed a lot more revealing than the black one she wore yesterday. Having gotten to the beach earlier to release some of the frustration he was feeling and clear his head, seeing her in a bikini even from a distance made his groin stir and after a few more waves, he decided to go in and spend time with her.

Watching her come out of the water was like seeing a water nymph come to life as water dripped from her body making her sparkle in the light and then when she went to squeeze water from her hair, it made her breasts jut out and he could see perfection hidden by tiny green triangles.

Even watching her dry off was just as arousing and as he jogged towards her, he couldn't help but note other men on the beach were also watching her with lecherous looks in their eyes. He made sure he got to her before any of those other holiday Romeos thought she was available…because she wasn't.

"Hey, you made it. Good swim?" he said, trying to keep his voice casual and jovial.

"It was great. How was the surf?" She gave him a bright smile as she sat on her towel, and popped her sunglasses and hat on.

"Great."

"Do you mind putting some lotion on my back, please?" She held out the bottle to him.

The memory of what happened yesterday made him hesitate, yet there was no other choice since he was the only one around to do it. Taking it and sitting behind her, he and poured lotion onto his hand and this time made sure that he briskly rubbed it on so she didn't have time to stress about it. She put lotion on the front of herself and then offered to do his back.

Her touch was so light and the way she skimmed her hands over his back was excruciating. At this rate, he was going to need to go for a swim to cool off.

She lay on her stomach reading her book and ignored him completely. He just lay beside her with his eyes shut and they were back to their comfortable silence.

After a while she rolled over and said, "I think I'll go for a swim."

"Great idea. I'll join you."

She tied her hair up again and they walked to the water together. They splashed each other before he grabbed her and dunked them both under the water.

"*Hey*," she pouted. "You've ruined my hair."

He smiled at this playful Montana.

"Sorry. Can I make it up to you?"

"How?" she said, coy.

"How about I let you dunk me?" His eyes twinkled as he moved closer to her. She jumped up with her arms on his broad shoulders to push him under but nothing happened except she slid down his body as he caught her around her waist.

"That's cheating." She pouted and he fell backwards pulling her with him. Standing them back up, he didn't release her but instead took her mouth in his. They both tasted salty as she wound her arms around his neck and pressed herself tightly to his chest.

He let out a moan and cupped her bottom so she wrapped her legs around his waist and she couldn't help but feel his arousal rubbing against her core. Suddenly the water seemed to be boiling around them as he untied her bikini top at the neck so he could lean her back and take one salty plump breast into his mouth making her moan as the waves lapped over her. His mouth moved to the other breast and the contrast between the heat of his mouth, the sun and the coolness of the water was so erotic that she could only cling to him with her legs tightly wrapped around his waist, her arms trying hard to hold onto him but she was losing focus because of what he was doing.

He pulled her back to him so he could claim her mouth with a demanding kiss. His hand moved down between them so he could rub her feminine centre as he moved her bikini bottom to one side and teased her with his fingers. Montana moaned into his mouth glad her eyes were closed and she couldn't see if anyone was watching, knowing what Lucas was doing to her — what she was letting him do. He inserted two fingers into her and she automatically clenched around him as he brought her to a peak, shattering the icy shell she erected around herself.

"God, you're amazing," he moaned, nibbling on her neck. "I want you so bad."

At those words, she knew she needed him too.

Right now.

No more thinking.

"Then have me," she whispered in his ear and a growl erupted from the back of his throat. A flurry of movement occurred as he nudged himself at her entrance and she waited for the pleasure.

"Look at me, Montana."

As she opened her eyes he slid so agonisingly slowly into her that her eyes widened and her mouth gasped at how stretched he was making her. She felt so full and started trembling.

"God, you're *so* tight," he said, breathing hard as he revelled in her facial features showing she found this just as exquisite as he did.

"Oh yes, I want more." Her breathing was just as shallow as his as she wrapped her legs tighter and he slowly started moving. The friction from the water and his hard erection was unbearable and it was all she could do not to come too soon.

Lucas lifted her up and down so she rubbed her body up and down his and soon her nipples were so sensitive, she couldn't wait any longer. As she went to yell her climax, he smothered her mouth with a kiss. Her orgasm was so intense he couldn't hold back and came with her. They were both panting and smiled at each other grateful they were in the water.

"Are you okay?" he said, concerned.

"It was perfect. I just hope no one saw us." She blushed pushing her face into the crook of his neck to hide as he looked around and saw everyone was oblivious to what they were just doing.

"I think we're fine," he said, as he gave her another lingering kiss and she tied up her bikini top and fixed herself while he did the same.

"I think I need to dry off," she said, as they left the water together hand in hand.

"I need another surf. I'll be back. Don't go anywhere."

He spun her around and gave her another thorough kiss before putting his wetsuit back on and grabbing his board. Whistling he headed back to the water.

Montana lay there feeling decadent and rejuvenated by what just happened. A smile was plastered to her face, unable to believe she just had sex in the ocean. She had never done anything like that before. Something about Lucas just carried her away. Although a little tender, she also felt so good and knew she was right in letting him touch her.

By tomorrow, she'd be a whole new Montana, ready to move forward but for now, she still had a whole night of Lucas and she smiled at the thought.

The sun was going down and they were still lazing on the beach.

"I have an idea," she said, as he kissed her shoulder and started moving up her neck.

"Uh-uh," he mumbled, nibbling on her ear.

"Why don't we watch the sunset and then the sunrise tomorrow?"

"Hmm, but what will we do in-between?" He pushed her down onto her back and covering himself over half of her, claimed her mouth once more as his hand went to her breasts and started to knead them causing her to tingle all over.

She let out a loud sigh, pushed him off and he sat up.

"Well, we'll have some dinner and then I can meet you in the morning," she said, deadpan but he saw the mischievous twinkle in her eye.

"Or I could just kidnap you for the night."

"There's no one here who would pay for my ransom," she said, feigning a worried look.

"Then I'll just have to keep you as my prisoner and have my wicked way with you."

The wolfish grin on his face made her shiver and she liked the thought.

"But there must be some way I can gain my freedom." She tried to swoon like a frail female, as she lay there propped up on her elbows.

He trailed a finger from her cheek down her neck to her breasts and swirled around over each piece of green material making her nipples pucker with desire.

"I'm sure that we can come to some sort of agreement," he grinned, before jumping on her again making her giggle.

They watched the sunset in each other's arms and as Montana leaned back into Lucas, she wished this moment could last forever. She didn't want to go back to reality.

Chapter Six

After agreeing Montana would check out of her hotel and move to Lucas' for the night, he made a few calls while he waited for her to pack. Now she wished for the sexy lingerie she hadn't brought.

Although his hotel wasn't far, it was more modern. When they arrived at the room they showered separately leaving her to wonder why he didn't ask her to join him.

Drying her hair and leaving it loose when she came out, a breath caught in her throat seeing candles lit all around the room and a table set up inside near the balcony door since the balcony was made for standing room only. Immediately she understood why he hadn't asked her to shower with him as the whole room was transformed into a romantic setting for two.

"Oh my. How did you get this all done so quickly?" she said, amazed at the sight.

"Champagne?" He held out a glass as she took it from him still trying to comprehend how romantic it all looked. "You look stunning."

She blushed at the compliment because she knew he was only being polite as she was only wearing a simple blue summer dress, but it didn't matter since they were in the room and no one was going to see her looking so plain next to him. Even in trousers and an open neck shirt, much the same as last night, he managed to take her breath away. His cologne, so spicy yet masculine, made her want to just hold him close so she could smell him.

While Montana showered, it had given Lucas a chance to think as he wondered about the change in Montana's personality today. This morning she seemed as distant as normal but then when they got to the beach, she was another Montana — sexy and playful.

His mind still boggled that she let him make love to her in the water when last night she was off-limits. Was it because her friends had departed and therefore she could indulge in a fling without them knowing? He didn't care what her reasons were since it was one of the best moments of his life when he entered her and shattered her icy shell. She was so incredibly tight and maybe that was the problem, she had been having a dry spell which was what made her skittish, he surmised.

It was one of the reasons for this private romantic dinner tonight, he was hoping to bed her again — all night. It had been a long time since he felt a really strong genuine connection with a woman. Part of him wondered if it was because he knew they were leaving tomorrow and lived in different hemispheres, that there could never be any chance of her getting the wrong idea and turning up on his doorstep unannounced looking for more. Deep down he knew it wasn't the truth, and was trying to keep the strange feeling he felt as far from him as possible.

They were enjoying a lovely dinner when Montana decided to have a little fun with Lucas.

"You know you and your cousins are the first, second and third Italians I've ever met," she said.

"Really?" he said, surprised.

"And your surname just happens to be Romero." There was a mischievous glint in her eyes. "I do hope that you're related to the Romero's pasta people."

"What?" He immediately tensed. "Why?" he croaked, his throat dry. Had he been wrong about Montana? Was she a clever little gold-digger?

"Because I *love* their pasta. Mum buys it all the time. I'd love to visit their factory and see what their secret is," she giggled, amused at the surprise on his face.

"*You like pasta?*" He knew he sounded idiotic, but this wasn't the conversation he thought he'd be having.

"Of course. I love it, doesn't everyone?"

Her teasing tone and smile finally penetrated his brain making him realise she was just being playful.

"*Really?*" he drawled, finally up with the play.

"I *am* Chinese," she said, proud. "*We* invented the stuff."

He looked like his perfectly handsome Italian head was about to spin around and explode and she tried hard to stifle her laughter at his expression.

"*You* invented pasta?" he said, incredulous as his eyes widened at the audacity of her statement. "That is the most ridiculous thing I have ever heard." He snorted for effect.

"Everyone knows Marco Polo was a big, fat thief who went to China and took our secret noodle recipe back to Italy."

"A terrible recipe that we Italians perfected over the thousands of years."

"Aha! So you admit you did steal it!" she said, victorious.

"I admit nothing."

"That's okay," she said, dismissively waving her hand. "We *all* know the truth."

She winked at him and although his blood was boiling, it wasn't with anger — a little irritation maybe and a whole lot of arousal for sure. This vixen fired his blood.

"And if I was one of those Romero's?" He arched an eyebrow in question ignoring her last comment and bring the conversation back to the beginning again.

"Maybe I'll seduce the pasta secrets out of you. Save me a heck of a lot of time instead of going to Italy to get them."

"So what you're really saying is that you want to see my noodle," he smirked.

"Only if it's al dente. I don't do wet and limp," she said, saucily and he was lost.

It was a little niggle that sat in the back of his mind all night. Knowing he would never see her again and he wanted, no, *needed* to get his fill of her before she disappeared.

His groin throbbed all night in anticipation of what was

to come. Unable to stand it anymore, he stood and hauled her to him making her give a squeal of surprise before their lips connected in a scorching kiss. His hands threaded through her silky hair as her arms pulled him closer so their bodies rubbed and she knew exactly what he felt and wanted.

Someone moaned, it may have been her, yet all she could do was hold him tightly as he teased and conquered her mouth with a desperation she had never felt before. Slowly he pushed her against the table so she sat on the edge grateful for the support, her legs opened to allow him to stand between them. Her hands somehow were moving to open his shirt, wanting to feel the heat of his skin, the hard contours of his muscular torso.

It was her dress which was irritating her, making it so she couldn't concentrate properly on Lucas. The bodice was pulled tight and felt so constricted because of the way she was sitting on it, limiting her movement, so she tried to lift each side of her bottom up to pull her dress to loosen it.

Lucas couldn't wait any longer. Knowing this was his last night with Montana, needing more than kisses and desperate to be inside her, without even thinking, he pulled her off the table, spun her around so she was now bent over it before flipping up her dress and roughly yanking her underwear down enough to be able to thrust deeply into her with a moan that revelled in just how tight, wet and hot she was for him.

She cried out his name in a gasp of pleasure and surprise, excited by his loss of control, spurring him on faster as he held her hips before unzipping the back of her dress and letting the bodice gape open. Her bra was then unclasped and soon Montana felt hot hands squeezing her breasts. His fingers rolling her nipples as she felt a blast of electricity shoot through her body to her vulva. It felt like it was stoking the furnace inside her, building it up to take her higher and higher. Just as he then roughly pinched, her body reared up as the first powerful wave of an orgasm flooded through her.

She was babbling incoherently as he came with a roar of her name before collapsing on top of her, panting hard.

Montana didn't know what came over her and she felt so deliciously naughty at being half undressed and taken over the table. She had never experienced sex apart from in a bed and so this was just as wanton and crazy as in the ocean. Both times with Lucas a bed was nowhere to be seen and it was sensational, she smiled to herself.

He let her up and as she turned saw the instant remorse on his face. Thinking that she was the one to blame she went to speak.

"I'm sorry. I didn't —"

"No," he forcefully said. "*I'm sorry*. I should never have treated you so appallingly. You're not...it was completely disrespectful of me and you deserved better."

She looked up at him with a smile and stroked his face gently, seeing the sincerity and contriteness.

"It was fantastic."

His face turned into a broad smile before bending his head to softly kiss her.

"Are you sure? I didn't hurt you?" he said, concerned and searching her face to make sure that she was telling him the truth.

His thoughtfulness touched her and just looking at him, so handsome, so sexy, just made her want more. She wanted him again — right now — the thought surprising even her.

Stepping away from him, she let her dress and bra fall to the ground, then stepped out of her underwear.

Lucas' eyes flared and he was instantly aroused again seeing Montana naked in front of him. When she pulled away, he thought he'd ruined their last night together even though she said what he just did was fantastic. What she said next almost made his head explode.

"Well, I'm not sure but maybe you could give me a very *thorough* examination just to make sure."

Not wasting any more time, he scooped her up into his arms and carried her to the bed.

"Oh, I will, but this time we use a bed."

She wasn't about to argue with her Italian god, but she was willing to scream down the room in ecstasy.

"Have you ever been to Italy?" he said, as they lay there enjoying the quiet.

"No. I haven't seen any of Europe. It's so far away from New Zealand and costs a lot just to get there. Even getting here was expensive. I'll go home and start saving again," she said, miserable.

"Why don't you come back to Italy with me and extend your holiday? I can show you the sights through the eyes of a native Italian?"

The thought of being so spontaneous and with a stranger terrified her and yet she wanted to laugh at how stupid a thought that was since Lucas knew her so intimately.

"I can't. I have a job I need to get back to and my family's expecting me home," she said, lamely.

Lucas just nodded. Even he was surprised he'd asked Montana to come home with him when she was supposed to be a bit of holiday fun — even if he knew from the moment he met her that she was different from any woman he had ever known.

Part of him thought that because her friends were in Europe, she might take him up on his offer, and her answer disappointed him more than he thought it would.

"Then I guess we have two choices: see the sunrise together like you suggested or spend every moment we have left in bed?" He left the choice up to her knowing that he'd be happy with either one.

"Let's see the sunrise."

"Would you mind if I have a surf?" he said, and she loved that about him. He really was a kind and thoughtful person.

"Of course not. It's your holiday too."

They both knew time was no longer on their side and wanted to spend as much of it as they could together so they spent all night in each other's arms sleeping in between bouts of sex before they got up and went down to the beach.

The wind was blowing a gentle yet cool breeze and Montana enjoyed being wrapped in Lucas' arms much like the last evening when they watched the sunset.

"Don't you wish we could stay here forever?" she sighed, trying to remember every detail of her time here, especially with him. "This place just seems so magical."

"Sì, but as they say, nothing lasts forever," he said, solemn.

She knew he was feeling the same sense of loss as she was, knowing they would be leaving each other in a matter of hours.

"It's beautiful, isn't it?"

"Sì, much like you," he said, making her smile.

"Thank you for last night, I'll never forget it."

"Me either."

It was the last words they spoke for a while, each lost in their own thoughts until the sun finished rising from the horizon.

Lucas saw the swells of the ocean and noted it was a perfect day for a surf. He needed it to help clear his head about Montana.

Montana could feel Lucas itching to go into the water. Twisting her head, she smiled.

"Go on, you know you're dying to go."

His smile was bright as he brought his lips down on hers. She put all her gratitude and thanks into her kiss making it as passionate as possible so he would know how much being with him meant to her.

Lucas was almost bowled over by how open her kiss seemed. The connection between them deeper than ever.

By the time they finished, they were both panting and Lucas almost suggested they go back to the hotel or have a quickie on the beach right now, but he needed time to process all the emotions swirling inside him.

"You'll be okay?" he said, standing ready to grab his board.

"Fine. I'll stay here for a while, but if I'm not here when you come back I'll be at the hotel," she said, hoping her lips weren't trembling and the tears wouldn't come.

"Okay."

He ran towards the surf and as soon as she saw him dive onto his board and begin paddling out into the ocean, she let the tears fall knowing she wouldn't see him again.

Sitting with a maelstrom of emotions swirling from head to toe as she watched Lucas, knowing he was enjoying himself, made her feel a little better.

She remembered back to that first morning she was sitting on the beach thinking of James. Now here she was again, but this time it was Lucas who filled her mind and heart. It may have only been a few days but meeting Lucas somehow changed her life forever. After sitting there for a while, she went back to the hotel and packed.

Lucas felt exhilarated and peaceful after having a surf. As he emerged from the water and noted he was alone on the beach, it didn't bother him although a little stab of disappointment shot through him that Montana wasn't sitting on the sand waiting, like when they met.

He thought back to that magical moment and smiled, it felt like he had known her all his life when in reality it was only a few days. While in the water he decided he was going to have to persuade Montana to come to Italy for a holiday or he was going to have to plan one to New Zealand. Either way, he was pretty sure even she would have to agree that whatever it was between them, it was something that needed to be explored further.

Exuberantly he opened the door to the room.

"Mon! You here?" he said, but the sound of silence was deafening. "Mon? Mon?" He anxiously looked around and noted that her stuff seemed to have vanished.

On the middle of the bed propped up by the pillows was a piece of paper with his name on it and a feeling of dread washed through him. He didn't want to open it, didn't want to know what it said and yet was compelled to do it.

Dear Lucas

I'm sorry to have left without a goodbye but I knew that I couldn't do it without crying. Even though we only met a few days ago, I feel like I've known you my whole life and I thank you for showing me such exquisite pleasure.

I'll never forget you.

Mon x

He didn't know whether to be angry or sad by her note and could see the teardrop stains on the paper and that made his heart squeeze.

As if on automatic pilot, he packed and left San Miguel...alone.

Chapter Seven

Montana cried all the way to the airport and on the entire flight from San Miguel, only stopping as it was announced they were three hours from their final destination of Auckland, New Zealand. She felt so guilty at leaving Lucas with just a note but what else was there to say? Sure, they could have had another round of amazing sex but then what? They'd still both be returning to their respective homes — on different sides of the world.

She already felt so silly at how truly close she had become to him after only knowing him for a few days. Poor Lucas probably would have thought she was crazy if she'd told him that. Then there'd be an awkwardness and she didn't want to see the relief in his eyes that their time together was finally over and he could get away from her.

Now he'd just think he had a lucky escape because she left first.

In her mind, it was the perfect ending watching the sunrise with him.

Now she was back in the bosom of her family and it helped to recharge her extremely flat and morose batteries. It also helped to slowly piece back together her broken heart.

The holiday to San Miguel did more than just give her a change of scenery, meeting Lucas fundamentally changed something inside her as well. Perhaps he managed to do the one thing no one else could — give her hope that her future might not be as bleak as she once thought.

A light rapping was heard on her door.

"Come in," she said, as the door opened and Indi poked her head in the room.

"Mon, do you want to talk?"

Montana waved her sister into the room and sat up on her bed making room.

Indi moved into the house after James died to not only give Montana company, but so she could also tentatively take the next step towards her own independence.

Since Indi and Montana were the two eldest siblings, they were extremely close and knew they could share their secrets with each other without fear.

To Indi, Montana may have returned home from her holiday seemingly lighter than when she left, however, when it was just the two of them, she couldn't help but notice her sister was miserable.

"Oh, Indi," she sighed. "My life is such a disaster."

Indi didn't say anything but just patiently waited for her sister to continue.

"My trip was…amazing, fabulous, wonderful," she said, trying to find the right word to describe it but even then, the words didn't seem to do it justice. "I met a guy, a hunk, a god even. He was…*super sexy*…h-o-t *hot*."

Montana broke into a smile just thinking about Lucas and wanted to laugh at how Indi's eyes looked like they were about to pop out of her head.

"*You met a guy?* Wow. Go Mon."

"Lucas was…exhilarating." Once again she was trying to find words to describe how she felt and knew Indi wouldn't judge her for jumping in the sack with the first guy she met. "He made me feel things I didn't even know I could." Sadness misted over her face. "Now I feel so guilty about James. How could I feel more for some random stranger than I ever had with James?" she whispered, as the tears began to flow.

Indi offered her a box of tissues and waited for her sister to calm down.

"It's okay, Mon. Maybe you were just caught up in the moment?"

"That's what I thought too. He made me lose control of my senses — myself — and I loved it."

"D-Do you love him?" Indi said, hesitant. She didn't know if you could possibly love a man after just knowing him for a few days — it seemed preposterous to her — but maybe if Montana had, then it couldn't be, because her sister wouldn't lie to her and it might go a way to explaining her sister's emotional upheaval.

"*Yes*, I think so," she said, in such a way leaving Indi in no doubt she had.

"So what happened?" It was more curiosity rather than concern because Indi had never seen her sister so wistful in her life, not even with James.

"I was sitting on the beach one morning and then this surfer came out of the water and sat beside me. At the time I thought why am I not freaking out over this and why would a complete stranger intrude on my solitude when there was a whole beach he could go and sit on. We pretty much sat in silence and it was weird and yet, I found it so comforting. Then later on, we were all at the beach and Izzy and Toni managed to attract these hot guys."

Indi laughed.

"It turned out that Lucas was actually cousins with both of these guys. Then Izzy's grandmother ended up in hospital so she rushed back to Spain. Toni went with her and so did Marco and Tonio, Lucas' cousins."

"Really? But you've all only just met."

Montana wasn't surprised to see Indi's confusion by the turn of events, if she hadn't lived it, she would be the exact same way.

"That's exactly what I thought too. I stayed behind because I had to come back home and Lucas kindly stayed to keep me company." She didn't add she also got mind-blowing sex as well, because she didn't want Indi to look at her like some kind of floozy that went out and slept with the first man she saw, which was pretty much what happened.

"That's why I purposely haven't emailed them although they've emailed me. I don't want to put them in the middle. Its better if they don't know anything, that way they can't get into trouble with the Romero boys," she said.

"Romero boys?" Indi giggled. "Sounds like they should all be Romeo boys, if you ask me."

Montana couldn't help but laugh at that.

"I don't think that you'd believe me if I told you."

Even though Indi was younger, Izzy and Toni hung out around the house so much Indi considered them family as well and wanted to know everything.

"Hey, I'm struggling with this whole conversation, what's a bit more. Lay it on me," Indi said and Montana told her story. "You're kidding me. Toni and Tonio? Antonio and Antonia? Well if that's not a match made in heaven, what is?"

Montana couldn't help but laugh at Indi's facial expressions.

"No, I'm not kidding but you're right. Honestly Indi, if you had been there you would have felt the electricity in the air between them all. It really was electrifying and as funny as it sounds, they actually did seem to fall in love at first sight." Once again there was that wistful note in her voice.

"Three cousins and three best friends all falling in love after basically meeting. What are the odds on that?" Indi said, incredulous, her head still spinning.

"I know. Freaky, right?"

"It must be the magic of San Miguel."

"The magic of San Miguel. That's the perfect analogy."

"I think I might have to go and holiday there. I know I could use a dose of romance," Indi sighed.

"Maybe when you're ready to fall in love, it's probably not for people who just want a hot fling," she teased, making them both smile.

A week later Montana was shocked to see one of her best friends standing on her doorstep in front of her.

"Toni, what are you doing here? When did you get back? What's wrong?" she said, instantly concerned while tightly hugging her best friend.

"Oh, Mon, it's all a big mess," Toni sobbed.

"Come on in and we'll talk." She ushered her friend inside the house.

Toni sobbed in her arms telling her everything that happened from the moment they left San Miguel.

Izzy's grandmother had a series of very small but thankfully non-life-threatening strokes which only added to everyone's worry.

After making sure Toni was okay, Tonio returned to Italy because he had work and it wasn't fair to make him stay especially since she was supporting Izzy.

"When Izzy's grandmother became more stable, Izzy and I took a quick trip to Italy to see the boys. I was so happy, even my parents were happy when I told them I thought I had met my future husband. Life was good and then…well, there was nothing for me to do and I had no money, so I came home," Toni sobbed.

"What did Tonio do or say?"

Montana silently prayed it was something heroic, but the fact her best friend was now sobbing in her arms made her realise it wasn't.

"That was it, Mon, he couldn't do or say anything except he loved me."

Montana tightly held her friend to her.

"I'm really sorry," she said, full of remorse.

The two women wallowed in their misery together with Montana telling Toni all about what happened with Lucas on San Miguel.

"Romero trouble?" Indi said when she came home and saw Toni, red eyed and blotchy faced.

Montana just nodded and Toni repeated in a condensed version of what happened making Indi just as sad.

"I guess it's true," she said.

"What?" Toni said.

"Misery really does love company. I'll get the ice cream," she grinned.

They laughed and followed Indi to the kitchen to get some ice-cream to cheer themselves up.

Lucas hadn't seen either of his cousins in a while because he didn't want to watch them all loved-up when he was still single and had nobody. Correction, the woman he wanted was now living on the other side of the world.

He kept to himself since returning after hearing his family talk about the wonderful women his cousins met, and made sure he was too busy working to be able to catch up with them.

Now it was his own mother telling him Tonio was down in the dumps. Alessia Romero urged Lucas to call his cousin and cheer him up.

Lucas, unsure of what happened between Tonio and Toni, did as his mother asked.

"I heard you were grumpy and moody," Lucas teased.

"Look who's talking. You're the invisible man," Tonio snorted.

He ignored the jab because it was true and this wasn't about him, but Tonio.

"What happened? I thought things with you and Toni were going swimmingly?" he said, concerned because as long as he had known Tonio, his cousin had *never* been grumpy.

"Toni left."

"What?" he said, stunned. "When? Why?"

"Because she was bored and had nothing to do here, and also had no money."

Now he understood and could sympathise with them both.

"I'm sorry. Is she planning on coming back?" And bringing Montana with her? he silently hoped.

"I don't know."

Lucas could hear Tonio slugging back the scotch.

"Have you asked her?"

"I'm not sure if I can. I mean, it's the same thing, right? What will she do?"

He felt just as miserable as Tonio, knowing that if by some miracle Montana came over to Europe, it would be the exact same thing. What would she do? Even if he gave her money, she'd still have to find ways to amuse and pass the time while he was working.

"I'm sorry, Tonio. I guess it would be the same thing with Montana if she ever came to Europe."

"Sì. So what happened between the two of you after we left? You've been holed up, and clearly are as miserable as me," Tonio said. "Did it not go that well?"

Before Lucas realised what he was doing, he was spilling his guts to his cousin, grateful it was over the phone. He didn't know if he could have said it aloud in person. It seemed to hurt too much. How could he feel so rotten after meeting a woman and only spending such a short amount of time with her?

It just made him think about how lucky he was Montana returned home. It could have been much worse if they spent more time together. Although…maybe they would have just fizzled out or would have it ended terribly, but something in his gut knew that was untrue.

Still, she was on her side of the world and he was on his.

Slugging back his drink in one gulp, he put the glass down and went back to doing some work to take his mind off Montana.

Chapter Eight

Montana was free! Free to do whatever she wanted…run around the house naked, twirl, scream and yell, eat, sleep, sit up all night, watching whatever she liked and it was going to be fabulous!

It didn't matter that she could do all that now, it just seemed even more exciting since she was about to go out into the big wide world — experiences unlimited — with so many people to meet and places to see. No one and nothing was going to stop her. Heaven help them if they did, she'd bulldoze them all down like toy soldiers. This was her life and her time.

Now if only she could remember where she put her passport then she'd be all set to go. Seriously, this couldn't be happening to her. After looking around her entire bedroom and even after she unpacked and repacked her suitcase, still that blasted passport could not be found.

"Mon, are you almost ready?" Indi called from downstairs.

"Almost!"

She didn't want to tell her sister she couldn't even find her passport since she'd spent so much time reassuring Indi and her parents she would be fine travelling all over the world, that she was responsible, sensible and above all, street smart.

Feeling flustered and slightly humiliated now she was about to dump the entire contents out of her handbag and suitcase for a third time when her younger brother, Boston appeared in the doorway of her room.

"Looking for something?" he smirked, leaning on the doorjamb.

"Go away! I'm trying to pack," she snapped.

"Really? Look's like you've finished to me," he mocked and that's when she realised he knew what she was missing. How?

"Get lost, Bos!"

"Okay, but you'll never find it," he chuckled, tapping a little book in his hand.

"Give that to me," she growled, lunging for it.

"Uh-uh. You keep saying that you're *so* grown up, but you lost your passport, *and* before you've even left the house," he teased.

"I didn't lose it. Obviously *you* stole it," she huffed, hands on her hips.

"Really? So where was it that I supposedly stole it from?" He arched his eyebrow in challenge.

Little brothers were such a pain in the butt sometimes.

"You obviously took it from my handbag," she confidently said, as he burst into laughter, irritating her even more.

"Doubt it, sis. *You* left it in the bathroom. Real responsible."

"Give it to me!"

"What are you going to do? Tell Mum? I don't think so."

She knew he was right, making her even more annoyed and irritated, if that was at all possible.

"What do you want?" she sighed, defeated and needing her passport.

"How about an, 'I love you, Boston. You're the best brother in the entire world and I'm going to miss you heaps'." He smirked as she gritted her teeth.

"I love you, Boston. You're the most annoying brother in the world and for some stupid and unknown reason, I'll miss you," she said, paraphrasing his words.

She held out her hand and he slapped her passport into it, grinning.

They hugged each other tight before shouting came from downstairs once more. Yelling back, she grabbed her suitcase and headed for the door.

A year had almost passed since San Miguel and now both Montana and Toni were winging their way to London. It had never been in Montana's original life plan to do an OE — overseas experience — like most other Kiwis, but since James' death and her bittersweet holiday in San Miguel, she felt like she needed a change of scenery once more and to just let loose.

Initially, her parents were concerned, but when they found out Toni was going with her, they seemed more reassured knowing their daughter would be with her best friend. Not to mention Izzy was also still in Europe although not in London, but now living in Italy with Marco — they were the only couple to have made it out of the three pairs.

It was such an exciting and yet daunting moment when they reached the airport but at the same time, Montana was ready to turn around and tell her parents this was a bad idea, that she had made a big mistake, and now didn't want to live on the other side of the world without her family.

However, her siblings were excited for her and they were already lining themselves up to stay with her when they came to visit on holidays, or as Indi would soon be doing her own OE she'd need a place to bunk down, and what were big sisters for if you couldn't mooch off them while you found your feet in a foreign country.

"I can't believe we're doing this," she said, as the plane began taxiing to the runway.

"I know. If it wasn't for Izzy's constant badgering and demolishing of all our protests and worries about being in a strange country and knowing no one, we'd still be at home safely tucked in bed."

Montana smiled at Toni's words. She was quite right about Izzy badgering them both to move to the other side of the world so that they could see each other more easily.

Izzy had worn them both down with a stubborn determination all her Spanish ancestors would have been proud of, and that's the real reason why the two best friends were now on a plane heading to the other side of the world, far away from their own friends and family.

Both Montana and Toni's protests about not knowing anyone and not having much money were soon bulldozed by the one-woman demolition crew that was Isabella Esteban.

It was Izzy who happily declared that she single-handedly solved their accommodation problems by having them stay with her cousin, Pedro who lived in London.

"Don't worry. Pedro is ecstatic at the thought of having two female housemates who are not only from New Zealand but my best friends," Izzy said.

Montana and Toni were more than a little sceptical by Izzy's declaration even if it did make them feel a little more safe and secure knowing that they would be living with Izzy's cousin, even though he was a stranger to them.

"I'm a little nervous. What happens if we don't like it?" Montana said.

Toni returned her best friend's sentiment as she too thought it would be exciting until she got on the plane. She felt the same reservations and nervousness about living so far away from friends and family.

"At least we have each other."

"Good point. And I'm sure that Izzy will visit at every chance she gets." Montana hoped they would get to see their friend more frequently. "Besides, didn't we agree we were going to travel everywhere and see as much as we could?"

A flicker of excitement rumbled through her once again and she felt a lot happier and relaxed.

"Yes, we were going to see the world and find us some *super hot* men on the way."

Toni's declaration made Montana giggle and her thoughts instantly drifted to Lucas.

Would she see him again? A small part of her hoped so. She couldn't deny she often thought of those few days with Lucas like it was a fantasy.

Toni too, couldn't wait to see Tonio again, to see if the chemistry they had, still burned brightly. Their communication dramatically slowed the longer they were apart and Toni knew for her part, it was because it was just too hard knowing how far away he was, living his own life and she wasn't a part of it.

Their excitement ramped up once again as soon as they began the approach to Heathrow Airport. This was it. They were finally in England and their reunion with Izzy at the airport was filled with shrieks of delight all round.

A very handsome man watched on amused as the three women continued to hug and talk over each other.

"Mon, Toni, I'd like you to meet my cousin, Pedro," Izzy said, after they finally calmed down.

"Señoritas, you are both as beautiful as Bella said. I can't wait to have you living with me. I've already got men lined up for you to date," he grinned.

"Izzy, what have you gotten us into?" Montana chided, trying to look shocked, yet she couldn't help but smile.

"Pedro, I asked you to let them stay and to look after them, *not* pimp them out," Izzy scowled.

"Who is Izzy?" Pedro looked confused.

"I am, you nitwit. Good grief, maybe it was a bad idea having you stay with him, he's clearly lost his marbles," Izzy teased, knowing her cousin would have never heard her called Izzy.

"Izzy? But everyone calls you Bella," he said, still bemused.

"We call her Izzy because over the years she had a few lapses in concentration, shall we say and so we used to tease her and call her Dizzy Izzy," Montana grinned.

"Mon!" Izzy wailed. "Why are you telling Pedro all my secrets? That's it, you're not staying with him now. I don't know what you'll end up confessing about me."

"Dizzy Izzy. I like that. And, it's true, *Izzy*, you are a little bit *dizzy*," he said, as he turned to Montana and Toni. "Did she ever tell you about the time she was trying to get into her car, she was furious the door wouldn't unlock or open until she realised it wasn't even her car!"

They all laughed but Izzy wasn't amused and turned pink at the story.

"Now look, you're telling my secrets," Izzy growled and stomped her foot, making the others laugh.

"I'm sure that we'll all keep that story to ourselves, right?" Toni grinned.

"Well, at least *for now*," Montana teased.

"Yes and who knows what interesting information we might learn about Pedro after staying there."

Now Pedro looked horrified and held his hand to his heart.

"You're right, Bella, these two can't stay with me. I can't have them sharing my deep dark secrets."

"You need to take them at least for a week, we can't leave them homeless, just yet. Mind you, should you want to dispose of the bodies, call me and I'll help," Izzy teased.

In the cab, Pedro was showing pictures on his phone to Toni and Montana.

"What are you doing, Pedro?" Izzy said.

"I'm showing the señoritas photos of my friends to see if they're interested in dating any of them. Although I have to say, can one of you at least go out with Colin? He's promised me his tickets to the football semi-finals if I set him up," he grinned.

"How do they know what we look like?" Toni said, curious.

"Oh, I showed them a picture Izzy had of all three of you in your bikinis. Let's just say, I suddenly had a lot of friends wanting to hang out with me while you're here."

"Pedro!" Izzy gasped. "That's creepy and wrong! They're my best friends. Don't make me call your mother and tell her what delinquent things you're up to."

"You see," Pedro sighed. "I do a favour for my favourite cousin and what do I get? Nothing in return. Just threats and blackmail."

Montana and Toni felt a lot more comfortable and relaxed once they reached Pedro's flat. They felt like they had known him for ages since he really was quite friendly and admitted he truly had been joking, well, except for Colin. He really would like those football tickets.

"I'm really sorry, Pedro, but I don't think that we know you well enough to be your sacrificial lambs for football tickets," Toni said, patting his shoulder.

He smiled muttering to himself.

"What did you say?" Montana said, curious.

"I said that God favoured me with two beautiful women landing in my lap, but then to teach me a horrible lesson, he's made them too strong to bend to my will," he grinned. "Just my luck." He snapped his fingers in disappointment as they all laughed.

"Don't worry, Pedro, I'm sure after a week, you'll be thanking your lucky stars that we're not only moving on, but didn't agree to date any of your friends, you may not have any friends left after we chew them up and spit them out," Toni chuckled.

"Izzy, you should have called Mario to have them. I can see I'll be the one moving as they'll take over my flat and leave my bags packed outside the door," Pedro said, feigning horror.

"Packed?" Montana giggled. "Oh no, we're not packing your stuff, we'll just throw it outside and you'll have to do all of that."

"What have I gotten myself into?" he groaned.

Everyone was laughing and having a good time getting to know each other, pleased they all seemed to have the same easy sense of humour.

Life in London was a whirlwind for the first few weeks as Montana and Toni did all the sightseeing they could before they got jobs. Pedro had kindly taken them under his wing and shown them how to use the Tube to get around, where all the shops were, and sent them off one day on a bus tour of London where they got to see all the major tourist attractions. Then he offered to take them away for the weekend since his girlfriend, Sally had a hen's weekend, so they went to see Stonehenge, Oxford and Cambridge.

"You know Pedro, it's a shame that you and Izzy aren't siblings. I think if you had come to New Zealand, the four of us would have had a rollicking good time growing up. I mean, you and Izzy are almost like identical twins," Toni said, as Montana agreed.

"That's why she's my favourite cousin," he said. "Except for when she blackmails me."

"I hear you," Montana said. "With my siblings, blackmail is almost a daily or at least a weekly occurrence. Someone always threatening to tattle something about someone else."

"How many siblings do you have?" he said.

"Five. Three sisters and two brothers. Then there were the adopted ones like Toni and Izzy, who just hung around like a bad smell and we couldn't get rid of them," she teased.

"Hey! Its not my fault I'm an only child and was desperate to have siblings so I borrowed yours," Toni laughed.

"Five siblings, wow, that's a lot. Its only me, my brother Mario and sister, Juanita." His phone beeped. "Oh, its Izzy wanting to know if I've killed you yet?" he chuckled.

"Tell her that you've buried us under Stonehenge as a sacrifice to the gods," Montana giggled.

"You know, it's taken a little while to think of Bella as Izzy but now that I have, I really like the name," he said, typing his reply. "She says that as long as she gets a share in any wealth coming my way, she won't tell a soul that you're missing."

"That's our Izzy," Toni laughed.

"She'll crumble as soon as my siblings get a hold of her. They can interrogate a person like a pro," Montana said.

"That is true," Toni said. "Phoenix is very unpredictable, who knows what he'd do to get to the truth."

"Yes, Boston will try to hold him off but Nix, well, he's not our family hot-head for nothing."

"Boston? Phoenix? These are your siblings' names?" He said it with a degree of surprise as Toni and Montana giggled.

"Yes. My parents travelled around America and loved it so much that they named us all after places over there," Montana smiled.

"Go on, tell him," Toni said.

They both liked to see the look on people's faces when they heard the names.

"Montana, Indiana, Boston, Phoenix, Alexandria and Savannah."

"Wow." Pedro's mind boggled.

"That's pretty much the same reaction we get from everyone," Montana laughed.

"Now will you two do a tour of Europe?" he said.

"I'm not sure," Montana said. "I mean is it better to do it before we get jobs or perhaps later in the year?"

"Perhaps you should see if you find a job first?" he said. "Maybe if you make some friends then they may want to travel to some places and you'll go with them. That's what a lot of people do."

"That's a great tip, thanks, Pedro. Perhaps we should do that, Mon. Wait and see what other people are up to first," Toni said.

"Okay, let's do that then. But in the meantime we can still do day trips around England or maybe even go up to Scotland or over to Ireland for a weekend," Montana said.

"But what about poor old Wales?" Toni laughed.

"Fine," she sighed. "We'll also go to Wales."

Neither of them said anything about Italy or how they might possibly be avoiding it.

Thanks to Pedro, both Toni and Montana had a nice flat to live in until they found jobs and could find their own place. Pedro kindly told them to take their time, that they were welcome to stay as long as they liked but his girlfriend, Sally wasn't terribly pleased her boyfriend invited two strange women to live with him even if they were his cousin's best friends.

Of course, Sally never voiced her displeasure out loud to Pedro or Izzy, when she called, but was forever dropping hints to the two women leaving them in no doubt that she wanted them gone — the sooner the better.

Toni got a job first thanks to her super efficient PA skills and she began temping until one of those companies decided to permanently hire her. Montana took longer to find a job, but she soon found one thanks to Pedro's connections, as a sales representative for The Food Boutique.

She had orientation for a week before they sent her out to various supermarkets and stores to peddle their new line of allergy friendly products they made under The Food Boutique, Tasty & Natural brand. It wasn't scintillating but it was a job and she actually enjoyed talking to customers although it wasn't always about the products she was supposed to be peddling.

Once their jobs settled down, the friends made a concerted effort to find a place to live much to Pedro's objections, but Sally's disdain for both of them meant they were glad to be leaving her behind. Both Montana and Toni had laughed at Sally's possessiveness over Pedro since he wasn't their type at all.

They had moved out of Pedro's a week ago when a knock at their door sounded. Both women looked at each other in alarm at who could possibly be knocking. Toni grabbed a wine bottle as a weapon as Montana nervously opened the door.

"Surprise!" the woman standing on the outer side shrieked to the two flatmates relief.

"Oh, thank God it's only you," Montana said, trying to calm her rapidly beating heart.

Toni discreetly lowered the bottle of wine at seeing their friend.

Izzy looked a little put-out at the reception they were giving her. She came all this way to surprise her two best friends and they seemed almost disappointed or was that relieved it was only her. Just who were they expecting?

"Just who did you think I was?" she said, annoyed before noting Toni trying to discreetly hide the bottle she was holding. Her eyes widened in understanding. "Did you think I was some kind of criminal?"

The two women remained silent unable to look their friend in the face.

"Sorry," they both mumbled.

"It's just such a shock to have you turn up unannounced," Montana said.

"That's why it's a surprise," Izzy said, rolling her eyes, but seeing her two friends looking contrite at their mistake, she forgave them as they had a group hug.

"Since that bottle of wine's out, you might as well open it and we'll christen your new place although I think Pedro is a little sad that you moved out." Izzy saw the silent look that her friends exchanged. "What?"

"Well…" Montana shifted uncomfortably, not wanting to cause problems for Izzy or Pedro.

"Sally hated us," Toni blurted out.

"What? Don't be crazy. She told me that you guys were like having sisters there," Izzy said, bewildered, yet knew her friends wouldn't lie to her.

"She said the same thing to Pedro, but when no one was around she'd kindly keep mentioning a ton of job vacancies, not to mention very affordable bed-sits that we might find of interest. Also she would keep asking us to remind her how long we were supposed to be staying with Pedro," Montana said, feeling awful and hoping that Izzy wasn't mad.

"Bed-sits? Gross." Izzy screwed up her nose. "Well, if that's true it's probably better that you left," she said, raising her glass of wine to toast her best friends. "Here's to an awesome adventure."

"It could have been even more awesome if the three of us were all single and able to go out and live it up, but alas, one of us had to get themselves a serious boyfriend," Montana teased.

"I guess that leaves all the hot guys for me and Mon," Toni said, as they all laughed.

They were all sitting and have a lively catch up when Montana noticed Izzy had a very sparkly looking diamond on her engagement finger.

"Is that what I think it is?" she shrieked, making Toni perplexed about what was going on as Izzy furiously nodded and held out her hand so her best friends could see.

"Marco proposed! I'm so happy *and* that's why I came here to surprise you, so you both could be the first to know."

Three grown women were now jumping around like they were ten years old having a slumber party.

"So will you two be my bridesmaids?" Izzy said, after all the exuberant celebrating calmed down.

"Well, that's a stupid question, like there is any doubt," Toni said.

"Yes, in fact, we would have been utterly devastated if you hadn't asked us," Montana smiled.

"Thank goodness I made the right decision then," Izzy said, rolling her eyes as they all laughed.

"We'll need smoking hot dresses," Toni said.

"What about me? I'm the bride, all eyes are supposed to be on me," Izzy pouted.

"Of course you'll be dressed as the sexy, sophisticated bride, who looks like a divine angel," Montana said. "But we want every other *single* man panting after us. I mean, it's not kind to have them panting after you since you're now permanently off the market."

"Yes, it's our job as great bridesmaids to cheer them up, distract them from their loss."

"It just shows what great friends you truly are to do all this *for me*," Izzy laughed.

"We can't help it, it is what best friends do," Toni grinned.

"I assume that Lucas and Tonio will be Marco's groomsmen?" Montana said.

"Like there was any doubt," Izzy said. "You okay, Mon? You've gone all quiet. Are you thinking about seeing Lucas again?"

"It sounds silly but I'm torn between nervousness and excitement at the same time."

"If it helps, I think he'll be happy to see you again too. He's been different since San Miguel according to Marco. He's lost interest in dating since Marco and I are together, although he and Tonio have been hanging out a lot which in turn sometimes makes Marco feel left out."

"Well, its not like Tonio's come running over here to visit me or anything," Toni said, depressed.

"Did you want him to?" Izzy said, curious, wondering if she needed to say something to Tonio.

"Yes and no," she sighed. "I mean, it would be kind of nice, but at the same time, its hard to know if we can just pick up where we left off, you know?"

The girls sympathised with their friend and they were all thoughtful knowing the change in anyone's relationship status was always going to cause an awkwardness between such close people.

Montana sat thinking of Lucas. Those last days together on San Miguel had been life changing for her. She hadn't expected it to change his life any but for her, being with Lucas bolstered her confidence and made her feel a little less alone, something she could never thank him enough for.

Every now and then, she thought of him and San Miguel and wondered if that was subconsciously part of the reason she agreed to do an OE. Had she been hoping to see Lucas again knowing that Izzy and Marco's relationship seemed to be going strong and wasn't surprised they were now engaged.

So maybe she somehow hoped they would all catch up again and then she wouldn't seem eager or desperate to reconnect with him. Maybe they could go on a date and if she was being honest, have another hot night of steamy sex.

No, she furiously shook her head to herself. It was a spectacular one-night fling that was never to be repeated. So what if Izzy said he didn't have a girlfriend, it didn't mean he was any more interested in her than she was in him.

It was the magic of San Miguel that brought them together. In reality, time had passed and he could in fact now be a jerk or she not his type and the thought saddened her. Now that Izzy and Marco were engaged, she squashed down all excitement and anxiety of seeing Lucas again.

"So have you and Marco set a date? How did he propose?"

"Oh, Mon, he was a total romantic, and I really was shocked. I truly hadn't been expecting it at all," Izzy sighed, as she recalled Marco's proposal.

By the time Izzy finished her story, Montana and Toni were both so happy and envious of Izzy's good fortune at the same time.

"You're so lucky and we're both *so* happy for you both. And, we might also be a teeny weeny bit jealous," Montana smiled.

"Don't worry, we're not getting married until next spring but the parents want us to have an engagement party. Actually we're going to have two — one in Italy and one in Spain because my grandmother can't travel. The one in Spain will be smaller and less formal. You can both decide which one you want to attend or both," Izzy said.

"That's a great idea. I can't wait to see your parents again and I also haven't seen any of either country," Montana said. "I'd better start working on a budget and how much time off work I can get."

"Me too," Toni said. "So how long are you staying here with us for?"

"I could only get to Sunday night."

"Then we'd better make the most of it."

The three women eagerly started talking all at once.

Chapter Nine

It was Marco's birthday and only Montana could make it to Italy as Toni was caught up in an extremely important work project requiring her to work long days and even weekends.

Wishing she didn't have to attend alone, Montana tried to beg off but Izzy steamrolled all her objections.

"How am I supposed to save to come to both of your engagement parties if I'm wasting money on a quick weekend to Italy now?"

"Don't worry, I'll organise you a ticket. You won't have to pay for a thing," Izzy said.

"But —"

"No buts, its done."

Once again the one woman bulldozer flattened Montana before she could even blink.

Knowing she was literally only going to be in Rome less

than twenty four hours, there also wasn't any time to sightsee due to her flight times which were the best Izzy could get since there was also a big football match on.

Izzy offered to have Montana stay the night but since the party was at their place, she didn't want to intrude as Izzy would have enough stress just organising it.

"Please Mon, can you pick up the cake?" Izzy said.

"The cake?"

"The shop's really close to the house, about a block but I can't get there in time with all this organising."

"Can't they deliver it?"

"They said they were short staffed because of the football."

Sighing, she had no choice but to agree.

"Sure."

"Thanks, Mon, I owe you one."

Montana hadn't planned her entrance to be like this, however, right now there was nothing she could do. Tears threatened as she nervously waited in the foyer by the front door. Her clothes, once pristine and definitely clean, were now covered in a mixture of water, dirt and sludge and stuck fast like glue to her body all because some jerk of a driver thought it would be hilarious to splash through the puddle in his racy sleek black Ferrari as he roared down the street.

She had just arrived at the shop to pick up the cake when it all happened so fast that she stood there frozen in shock for about ten minutes. Her brain obviously short-circuited because she just didn't know what to do.

Even the people in the shop were aghast at what happened

to her and no amount of napkins could clean up the mess she now was.

The only luck she seemed to be having was that the rain had stopped earlier, but it was an exercise in futility to get a taxi as there were none around because of the football and knowing it wasn't possible to go and change, she now not only had to walk but would be late as she squished and trudged her way to Izzy and Marco's house. Hot salty tears steadily streamed down her face but she didn't dare wipe them off just in case she smudged more dirt or accidentally dropped the cake. Tiny bits of her dirty clothes were beginning to dry and get that hard and stiff material feeling.

By the time she got to the address, her crying was overtaken by anger. Feeling very cold and stiff from the way she walked and the way her arms bent at an awkward angle from holding a fairly heavy box for a long time, she somehow managed to press the doorbell.

When Izzy got to the foyer and saw her friend looking bedraggled and worse than something the cat dragged in, she elicited a gasp of horror.

"Dios mío, what on earth happened?"

Izzy took the very heavy feeling box so Montana could finally be free of the extra weight but it was too late, her arms were aching.

Luckily, since they were in the foyer, no one else could see the state she arrived in, Montana thought with relief.

"Come on, let's get you out of those things. You can shower and I'll lend you something," Izzy said, ushering her to the bedroom.

Gingerly Montana followed her friend who fussed and found her a couple of dresses to choose from.

"The only shoes that might be okay are these," Izzy said, holding up one red and one black shoe. "Yours are soaked. I'll come back later so take your time, don't rush."

Looking at herself properly in the mirror, tears fell at the mess of a person that stared back. Her blouse was utterly ruined and she threw it in the bin. The skirt was just as bad and followed the blouse to its demise. Only her underwear had been spared.

Turning on the shower, she hopped into the cubicle trying hard to wash all the dirt off her face and out of her hair. Standing under the hot stream of water, it took her body a while to heat up and also her arm muscles to relax.

Feeling much better, calmer and relaxed, she slipped into one of Izzy's designer dresses and was silently thankful Izzy hadn't picked any that were too fitting because she wasn't as svelte as her friend.

As it was, the black dress was a bit of a tight squeeze in the bodice area but the skirt part flowed over her hips. Staring at herself in the mirror she looked almost voluptuous she giggled to herself.

There was a quiet knock on the door.

"Mon?"

"Come on in, Iz."

Montana couldn't help but laugh at Izzy's face upon seeing her. Her friend's eyes had almost popped out of her head.

"Holy moly, Mon. You look absolutely gorgeous."

"It's your dress, Iz. I hope I haven't stretched it too much."

"Who cares? Keep it. You look fantastic."

"How was the cake?" she said, hesitant.

"Its fine. Thanks for getting it again, Mon. I'm sorry that it got you all wet."

"It wasn't your fault some jerk in a flash looking Ferrari thought it would be funny to splash through a puddle like a racing car driver the exact same time I was outside the shop although, if I saw him, I'd be giving him a piece of my mind."

"About that…" Izzy went quiet.

"What? What is it?"

"I think I might know who the jerk is that splashed you. He's here tonight and I'm sure that it wasn't done on purpose."

"What? Who?"

"I'll tell you after dessert. The last thing I need is for you to start throwing cake around," Izzy teased, but there was an undertone of anxiousness in her voice.

"Dessert? Have I been that long? I'm *so* sorry, Iz," she said, contrite.

"It wasn't your fault, Mon. I've put some dinner aside for you. Come and have dessert first."

"Is this the European way? Dessert before dinner?" she teased, hoping to relax Izzy.

"Only for you, Mon," her best friend grinned.

They entered a large room and Montana wasn't sure if this was a lounge or a ballroom since it seemed not only very large but there were a lot of people everywhere.

Izzy left her to go and find Marco and so she stood like a wallflower at the back unable to contribute to the conversations swirling around her since they were all in Italian.

Feeling self-conscious she smiled at people when eye contact was made but the longer she stood there alone, she began to wish she hadn't come, or that Toni could have also made it.

A couple of waiters were circulating to ensure everyone had a full glass of champagne and Montana was relieved to have something in her hand but resisted the urge to drink as her stomach growled in hunger.

Embarrassed, she discreetly looked around to see if anyone in near distance heard, but everyone seemed oblivious to her relief.

Izzy's voice rose above the din and everyone stopped talking and turned to look at their hosts. Montana couldn't see past or over everyone so she just strained to hear Izzy's words about Marco before she heard her friend excitedly squeal, "Happy birthday!"

Everyone clapped, cheered and toasted the birthday boy and Montana politely took a sip of champagne.

Marco responded with thanks and declarations of love to his beautiful fiancée before everyone toasted Izzy and the room was advised to enjoy cake and dessert from the buffet.

Not knowing where the buffet table was and not wanting to move from the doorway, Montana remained where she was.

"You haven't moved an inch," Izzy chided, finding her friend exactly where she left her.

"Sorry Izzy, I don't really fit in. I don't speak Italian or know anyone," she said, embarrassed. "I wish you had told me that this was going to be a huge party. I thought tonight was just us for dinner." She sounded childish, but felt like a fish out of water and couldn't hide how uncomfortable she was.

"Sorry, Mon." Izzy gave her an apologetic look. "You're right, I should have told you, but I knew you wouldn't have come since Toni isn't here."

Her best friend knew her too well. She wouldn't have come for the aforementioned reason Izzy just said. Maybe getting drenched had been a good thing after all.

"Did you even need the cake?" She looked suspiciously at Izzy.

"Yes and no." Izzy flushed. "Yes, because it's to surprise Marco with tomorrow at his family's celebration dinner but no, I could have gone and picked it up tomorrow. I'm really sorry for tricking you, Mon."

"It's okay, it's not your fault you know me too well. I'm sorry, Iz but can I get something to eat, I'm starving." Her stomach loudly growled and she reddened as Izzy laughed.

"Come on, let's go to the kitchen and we can have peace and quiet in there." Izzy led her by the hand. "Let me reheat it for you," she said, putting the plate into the microwave.

"It's fine, Iz. You go and enjoy your guests. I can manage." Montana felt guilty for taking her friend away from all of her guests.

"If you're sure…"

"I'm a big girl. I think I can manage."

"Okay but you can't go until we've talked…properly."

"We'll see," she teased.

"Mon…" Izzy warned.

"You'd better get, Iz before everyone comes in here looking for you."

Torn between wanting to make sure her best friend didn't do a runner and needing to be a good hostess, Izzy reluctantly left the kitchen.

Montana enjoyed her meal and was putting her plate under the tap to rinse when she heard the kitchen door open and men's voices entering.

"She's a dream. A powerfully fast car that just purrs."

"So you did buy the newest Ferrari on a whim? Is it red?"

"It wasn't a whim, well okay, it was. But no, it's black, a bit more understated," the man chuckled. "Although I got it all dirty by driving through some puddles on the way here tonight."

She scowled to herself at the man's remark that he almost sounded upset his precious car had gotten dirty, never mind the drenching the jerk gave her.

"Can't wait to check it out, dirt and all," the other man said, before realising there was someone else standing in the kitchen with them. "Montana, so good to see you again. I'm glad you could make it." Marco smiled, hiding his surprise at her appearance.

"Thanks," she said, but all her focus was on the sexy handsome man with him.

"Montana, always a pleasure," Lucas said, but the gleam in his eyes flickered with the memory of their last meeting in San Miguel.

Annoyance shot through her and as Lucas went to greet her, she automatically raised her hand and slapped his face as hard as she could before she could even think about what she was doing.

"So you're the jerk who splashed me!" she snapped, as two stunned faces looked back at her.

Silence engulfed the room.

"I'm sorry. I hadn't realised," he said, contrite, his face red and taking a step back before he moved his hand to his cheek to rub it.

"No, you wouldn't have, would you," she berated, unable to stop herself.

"I think I hear Izzy calling my name," Marco said, exiting the kitchen as fast as possible leaving his cousin and fiancée's best friend alone. He could only hope they didn't kill each other.

"You look beautiful," Lucas said, in an attempt to calm her down and maybe distract her train of thought but the truth was, she was more than beautiful standing there with anger blazing in her caramel eyes. Her dress made her look like she was a siren tempting sailors and he was willing to jump in feet first.

If it was at all possible, she looked even more gorgeous than when he met her on San Miguel. She looked so alive and his eyes kept being drawn down to her chest, the outline swell of luscious breasts he once suckled, touched, nipped and massaged. Shifting his stance because his arousal was now awake, he was thankful the kitchen island was hiding him from her sight.

The huskiness in Lucas' voice made Montana want to throw herself at him. She knew he was looking at her cleavage and it made her tingly with the memory of his very clever mouth on her breasts and just standing in his presence again, she felt the same strong attraction she felt on San Miguel.

"No thanks to you," she rebuked, once more remembering what happened earlier tonight.

He ignored her irritation at him.

"Why are you in the kitchen hiding? You should be out there —"

"Because I missed dinner thanks to your idiocy. Thankfully, Izzy was kind enough to put a plate aside for me."

"Well you don't look like anything untoward happened. In fact, you look like a model."

He had an almost wolfish look on his face as he gave her a very thorough assessing look from her head to her toes that were curling, earning a silent curse to herself for even reacting to it. Still unable to contain herself, she erupted again.

"Once more, it's no thanks to you! I *had* to borrow a dress from Izzy since you made me look worse than something the cat had dragged in!"

She stubbornly refused to mention he had actually done her a favour because showing up with what she had been wearing meant she would have felt even more horribly out of place and embarrassed.

"I guess I owe you new clothes and dinner," he said.

The glint in his eye made her bite her bottom lip sensing it was like a friendly harmless offer when it was really a wide open, well laid camouflaged trap she would be walking into. Just as she opened her mouth to reply, the kitchen door swung open and a giggly woman entered.

"Lucas, honey, here you are," the woman said, coming over to his side and pressing herself into him. "Baby, I'm hot and horny. Can we leave now?"

Although she thought she was whispering, it was loud enough for everyone to hear and even though Montana quickly averted her gaze, she knew exactly where the woman's hand went, as it was hard to ignore her giggle of appreciation.

"Mm, I guess you're ready for me too."

Montana took the moment's distraction as a chance to escape as Lucas muttered a curse at Raquel's intrusion. He only brought her tonight to fend off any other potential women on the prowl. Over the past year he rarely dated and there had definitely been no girlfriends.

As floored as he was to see Montana at Marco's party especially since his cousin hadn't mentioned she was coming, but damn, if Montana's sudden appearance not only put a dampener on his night with Raquel but he felt the guilt churning in his stomach that Montana thought he had moved on with someone as vapid as Raquel.

The truth was, ever since he heard she and Toni were living in London and knowing that even Tonio hadn't gone to see Toni yet, it made him feel a lot better he hadn't seen Montana.

Now seeing her tonight, all he wanted was for them to be in his bed naked and her screaming his name again.

Montana escaped back into the party to disappear in the throng of people hoping Lucas couldn't and wouldn't find her. Keeping an eye on the room, she finally relaxed when Tonio found her.

She hadn't seen him since San Miguel, but he still looked dashing and wore the sunniest of smiles on his face when he recognised her.

"Montana, you look beautiful. It's been too long," he said, giving her an exuberant hug as he lifted her off her feet and she gave a little squeal. "How have you been?"

"Great, and you?" She sounded irritable and blamed her earlier altercation with Lucas on her mood. The smile fell off his face at her tone and she felt instantly guilty. "Sorry, I shouldn't take my annoyance at your cousin out on you," she said. "So how have you been?"

"Good, good," he said, before his voice lowered. "How is Toni?"

She saw the flicker of interest in his eyes and wished Toni could have made it.

"Great, although I have to be honest, even I haven't seen much of her lately. We're like ships in the night since she's really busy at work at the moment, otherwise she would have been here."

The look of relief on Tonio's face at her answer made Montana realise he thought Toni hadn't come because she was avoiding him.

Chatting and catching up like old friends and having a good laugh was how Marco found them.

"Happy birthday, Marco," she brightly said, giving him a hug and kiss. "Sorry I didn't say it earlier."

"Quite all right. You had other things on your mind."

She flushed and everyone was now looking curiously at her.

"I found out who splashed me," she said, in a quiet voice so only Izzy, who just joined them, could hear.

The two friends didn't need words, the look explained everything to them although she could tell Izzy was dying to know the details.

"It's been a great night," she said.

"It sure has," Marco said, kissing his fiancée. "Now that everyone's left, does anyone want coffee?"

Montana looked around the room and realised Marco was right, there was only a handful of people left and even those people were getting ready to leave too. Thankfully she couldn't see Lucas and his date either.

"Don't worry, he's left," Izzy said, confirming Montana's thoughts as she exhaled the breath she wasn't even aware she had been holding in.

"Coffee sounds great."

"Yes, now we can have a real catch up."

Izzy's tone may have sounded casual, but Montana knew her friend meant she wanted all the juicy details about what Marco alluded to only minutes prior.

"It's time for me to head off as well," Tonio said, and Marco looked a little disappointed. "I'll catch up with you guys tomorrow night for dinner though."

"Definitely." Marco perked up at the thought.

After saying goodbye to everyone, the three remaining people went into the kitchen.

"So spill," Izzy said, not beating around the bush. She wanted details and she wanted them now.

"Well, I was talking to Tonio and then —"

"Mon!" Izzy wailed in frustration and Montana couldn't help but laugh at her best friend's impatience.

"Fine, but it's really nothing exciting," she said, explaining the whole story with Marco's version of what happened at the beginning in the kitchen before she slapped Lucas and Marco made his quick getaway.

"Maybe I should have told you it was Lucas earlier on," Izzy said, ruefully biting her lip.

"Why? I still probably would have kicked him in the shins, after all he did splash me and ruin my clothes," she said, making Izzy smile.

"*Bella*, I might head for bed. Don't be long, okay?" Marco said, to his fiancée with that heat in his eyes making Montana envious.

Marco always called his fiancée Izzy in private or somewhere casual otherwise he called her Bella like her family and friends and Izzy loved the distinction. However, every time she heard him say *Bella* with a huskiness in his voice, she knew he wanted her and it made her tingle all over. But right now, she brushed those sexual thoughts aside to focus on her best friend.

Chapter Ten

Hours later, Montana yawned and noted the time was almost two in the morning. If she had realised catching up with Izzy would be all night, then perhaps she should have just stayed with her friend. Alas, as it now was, she'd make it to her bed for a few hours of sleep and then be back on the plane.

A light knocking on the front door sounded.

"That must be the taxi," Izzy said. "Lucas? What are you doing here?"

They were both surprised to see Marco's cousin on the other side of the door and not the taxi driver.

Montana wanted to groan. Why would Lucas be here and at this time of the night? Shouldn't he'd be rolling around in bed with his girlfriend?

"Marco thought Montana might need a lift. He wanted to make sure she got back to her hotel safely," Lucas said, sheepish.

Montana silently cursed Marco and while Izzy might have been slightly annoyed with her fiancé about doing such a terribly blatant thing, she agreed with it.

"Oh, we've ordered a taxi so —" Izzy said

"Actually I just sent him away," Lucas said.

"What? You had no right to do that," Montana said, furious.

"Too late," he grinned. "So do you want the lift or did you want to walk?"

"I'll walk thanks," she said, stubborn. There was no way she was getting into a car with him.

"I'll even let you drive." He dangled the key in front of her face.

She noted the horse on the keyring and looked past him but it was too dark to make out the car, so she just assumed it was the same offending one.

"You'll let me drive." She snorted her disbelief.

"Why not? It's well after midnight, the roads won't be busy so it's unlikely you'll hit someone," he teased, making her bristle.

Her arm shot out and punched him hard on the arm but he didn't even flinch.

"There, I hit you," she snapped, snatching the key from him and stalking off to the car.

His chuckle didn't help her mood nor did Izzy's cheerful words of farewell.

As Montana got into the car, she thought she was sitting in the rear since the seat was right back due to Lucas' long powerful legs. Stop it! she berated herself. Don't even think about things like that. Think about how annoying he is.

It didn't help that he was all too happy to tell her how to move the seat forward.

This really wasn't a good idea, she thought as he adjusted the passenger side to fit his long frame into the vehicle. It felt far too cramped with him being beside her.

"Couldn't you have gotten a bigger car?" she said, irritable.

"What? You don't find this *cosy*?" he teased, his eyes twinkling.

"Save it for your girlfriend. I can't believe that you'd do Marco's bidding at this time of the night."

"She's not my girlfriend."

"Fine, your bed buddy then," she huffed.

"She's not that either."

His answer made Montana pause as she pretended she was looking for how to turn the lights on and not seem relieved Lucas hadn't slept with his date. She shouldn't even care whether he did or not, but the fact he didn't eased the tension in her.

The car was way more powerful than anything she was used to and just putting the weight of her foot only slightly on the accelerator made it take off faster than she anticipated. The fact she was wearing heels didn't help either. The wheels spun quickly like a race car on the starting line and Montana wondered in embarrassment if she had just left lasting tyre marks on Marco's driveway.

"Whoa," he said, immediately gripping the dashboard tightly as she came to terms with the car. Maybe this was a terrible idea, he panicked. He wanted to get to her hotel in one piece and if he had been thinking straight he would have gone home and changed cars, but he had been at the office instead of having a hot night of sex with Raquel as originally planned, all because of the woman sitting beside him.

He hadn't known Montana was going to be at Marco's tonight. Marco couldn't have known either because he was sure his cousin would have mentioned it. However, seeing Montana again, and in that dress, he was instantly aroused and could still feel the electricity flow between them even though it had been a year since he met her and spent that incredible night on San Miguel.

After she fled Marco's kitchen he tried to find her but couldn't through the throng of people until he finally saw her with Tonio. Instead of going over and joining the conversation like he wanted to, he decided it would probably be better to leave, take Raquel home and then return. It wasn't until he dropped a very disappointed Raquel home that he realised returning to Marco's still wouldn't ensure a very warm reception from Montana and so he went to the office to do some work to take his mind off just how sexy and compelling Montana still was.

Now he finally had her alone but the fear of a car crash consumed his mind. Letting her loose behind the wheel of such a powerful car hadn't been his brightest idea but then, he wasn't thinking past the fact he only wanted to be alone with her.

"She was only a date and Marco was just concerned that's all," he said, as she shot him a look of disbelief.

Although he was only slightly more relaxed being on a straight road knowing they were only going in a straight line, most of the better hotels were located behind them.

"Ah, where are we going?"

Marco told him Montana apparently trudged completely soggy to their place and he felt guilty about it. However, being kidnapped by a woman who was driving a powerful car she wasn't used to, made him very nervous indeed.

"Since I'm never going to ever drive something like this again, I thought I'd better make the most of the opportunity especially since as you say, there's not much traffic around either," she grinned, putting her foot down harder on the accelerator.

"Any speeding tickets, you have to pay for," he said, and she eased off the accelerator much to his relief.

"Killjoy."

In the darkness of the car, he smiled to himself at her reply.

"Listen, I really am sorry about splashing you and ruining your clothes," he said, as she felt a hard horrible whack from her guilty conscience as it kicked her.

"Don't worry about it, you actually ended up doing me a favour," she mumbled.

"What's that?" he grinned, leaning closer as if he hadn't heard.

His nearness was ruining her concentration and so she pushed him back onto his own side of the car with her arm and he reluctantly yielded. She pulled the car to the kerb and turned to face him.

"Izzy didn't tell me it was a big fancy party. If you hadn't splashed me, I would have stood out like a sore thumb in my casual clothes."

Oh, she would have stood out all right, just not for the reasons she thought. She would have been a beacon in the crowd to him and he would have noticed her straight away and not been taken by surprise at her appearance.

She turned the car around and once again they sat not moving but facing the direction they came from.

"What's wrong?" he said, seeing the frown on her face.

"I don't know where my hotel is," she laughed. "I was so caught up in driving that I have no idea where I am. I mean, I know we've only driven in a straight line but still…"

"Why don't we switch places and I'll drop you off," he said, relieved.

"Did my driving scare you that much?" she teased.

"Yes."

"I guess we'd better switch then, but only because I'm pretty sure I'll never get back to the hotel without hitting something," she sighed.

She felt him tense at the thought before he quickly alighted so she couldn't change her mind.

It was actually harder to get out of the car than in it and she waited until Lucas came around and offer her a hand when suddenly she found herself in his arms.

Looking up she knew she wanted to kiss him again, but her nerves flared so she quickly moved to brush past him squashing down the urge.

Lucas loved even that tiny moment of having Montana briefly in his arms again. It reminded him of San Miguel and it would have been so easy to just bend his head and kiss her but he let her go because he knew that although he was desperate to kiss her, it wouldn't have been enough and the side of the main road wasn't the place for what he wanted.

She couldn't help but giggle as he tried to sit awkwardly in the car and move the seat.

"I think you've cut me in half," he moaned.

"That'll teach you for having long legs."

Once he managed to adjust everything back to suit his driving, he looked at her.

"Right, want to see how to really drive a car like this?"

"Okay, hot shot, dazzle me," she said, as he gunned the motor.

They sped back down the road much faster than she drove and it hadn't taken much time to be back at the start when flashing lights and a siren sounded behind them. Lucas groaned and Montana burst into laughter.

Watching Lucas get out of his car to talk to the officer, the only thing Montana could hear was the contriteness in his voice. Having no idea what he was saying, she could only imagine he was apologising for being a macho male trying to show-off his car to impress a lady.

"Not a word," he growled, climbing back in holding the speeding ticket, but she was too busy laughing to even speak.

"So ironic," she said, between the fits of giggles and wiping the tears away from her eyes.

"It's not funny," he growled in mock anger.

"No, it's not funny…it's totally hilarious. Did you tell him that you were showing off for my benefit?"

Another growl from the back of his throat had her in fits of laughter again.

He pulled up to her hotel and luckily there was a doorman to help her out of the car.

"Thanks for the lift, speedy. Maybe I'll catch you around sometime or not, depending on how fast you're going," she teased, before quickly walking inside before he even had a chance to say goodnight or even better, see her to her room where a goodnight kiss or more had definitely been on the cards.

Frustration rolled through him as he zoomed off before remembering his ticket and slowing down.

Lucas walked into the hotel reception with a determined stride, looking every inch the devastatingly handsome man he was. His designer suit fitted perfectly and to anyone looking, they could see he was a man of importance just by the way he walked and wore his clothes.

The woman behind the desk couldn't help but stare at such a fine specimen of a man.

"Can you please give me the room number of Montana…" A frown crossed his face as he realised he didn't even know her surname. Had she ever told him?

As he lazily lent on the desk he noted the woman was dazzled enough by him not to even be aware of his mistake as she took a minute before she comprehended his words.

"I'm sorry but Ms Chan has already checked out," the woman said, thinking that Ms Chan was lucky to have such a hunk asking for her room.

"Are you sure?" he frowned.

She checked again.

"Yes, sir."

Damn, he thought irritably to himself. He thought he was clever dropping in to surprise Montana and whisk her off for lunch, that he hadn't even thought about a scenario where she had already departed and silently cursed himself for not asking just how long she was staying in Rome.

A slow smile then appeared on his face as an anticipation he hadn't felt in a long while rolled through his body. He always enjoyed a challenge and after seeing Montana again, he knew he was going to find her once more. The best place to start was with Marco. Yes, his cousin would tell him all the details he needed to know and then he would have Montana back in his life and more importantly, in his bed.

Montana returned to London and filled Toni in on what she missed, trying hard to hide the smile at Toni's eagerness to know about Tonio.

"So?"

"So what?" she said, nonchalant.

"*Mon*," Toni wailed. "Tell me!"

"Well, since you asked…Lucas is still *hot* —"

"Mon! If you don't hurry up and tell me about Tonio, I'm going to sit on you and box your ears," Toni growled.

She heaved a heavy sigh and then laughed.

"Oh fine, but it was fun teasing you. If you must know, Tonio missed you. It really was a shame you couldn't make it. I also wouldn't be surprised if he turned up on our doorstep unannounced."

Suddenly there was a knock at the door and both women's eyes went wide in shock.

"You don't think…"

"Surely not."

Toni rushed into her room and Montana slowly counted to ten before going to the door. Opening it, she was stunned to see a man holding a bunch of flowers.

"Delivery for Antonia Patterson."

"Thanks," she said, taking the flowers. "Toni! There's a delivery for you."

Toni came out of her room, saw the flowers and smiled.

"Who would be sending me flowers?"

"Read the card."

Plucking the white card out of the flowers, Toni read it and sighed.

"They're from Tonio saying he's sorry I couldn't make Marco's birthday."

"That's so sweet. Somehow I don't think you have to worry about Tonio's feelings anymore," she giggled.

Placing the flowers in her bedroom, Toni came out and badgered Montana for the rest of the details especially about her altercation with Lucas.

Chapter Eleven

As Izzy was having two engagement parties, Montana and Toni decided they would go to both and use it as a chance to also see some of Europe. Montana was looking forward to seeing some more of the world and felt like a butterfly, flitting from one exotic place to another.

When they went exploring around the UK, she sometimes wished James was here to join her adventure and yet they had both been happy in New Zealand. Travelling the world hadn't been even a twinkle in their future. They both just wanted to be married and have children.

That part saddened her the most — the fact they never had children — although, sometimes she felt guilty at being relieved they hadn't, since it would have been even more devastating to know their child would grow up without its father.

She also felt guilty about not changing her surname to her married name before James died. It was always on her list of things to do yet she never quite got around to it and James hadn't minded in the least. Now every time she went to book flights or hotels — things that weren't already set up — which asked for her surname, it hit home more that her surname was still Chan and not Dobson.

Because of Toni's job, she had a tight time-frame and could only manage an extra day off work for their Spain trip whereas Montana managed to get two. Since Toni had previously been to Spain, they decided to see things Toni missed and therefore Montana could see anything else after Toni returned to London.

Finally they were on their way to Spain for Izzy's first engagement party.

"I'm so nervous," Toni said.

"Why? You've been there before."

"Because Tonio's going to be there. This is the first time that I've seen him since I left."

"Oh." She knew they had been in contact since he sent Toni flowers. "Where are you meeting up?"

"At the hotel."

"*Really?*" She arched an eyebrow, trying hard to suppress her laughter. "I guess I should just play the weekend by ear then. I'm happy to sightsee by myself."

"What do you mean?" Toni said, puzzled. "I thought we were sightseeing together."

"You're meeting Tonio *at the hotel*. Hello? Even I know what that means," she giggled.

"Oh." Toni instantly went beet red. "I'm sure that —"

"Don't make promises you can't keep. Don't forget it's been ages since you've seen him and you both have *a lot* of catching up to do."

"Well, that's true," Toni grinned. "But I do really want to go sightseeing as well."

"Like I said, I'm happy to play it by ear, but if you could just give me advanced warning of your plans so I can sort myself, I'd appreciate it."

As soon as they reached the hotel, Tonio was already there waiting on the other side of the reception area and the look exchanged between the couple was electric.

"I'm not expecting you to join me tomorrow at all," Montana said, grabbing her room key.

"I think you're right. I'm melting inside and I've only laid eyes on him. Thank God, he's standing miles away," Toni said.

"I think I'll let you both go up in the elevator alone, otherwise it could get a little awkward."

"Thanks Mon."

"Have an orgasmic night."

Toni laughed and excitedly skipped over to Tonio who was not only brightly smiling but his eyes smouldered with desire. Watching the couple made Montana envious at the joy radiated on Toni's face. Sighing, she followed alone.

The next morning she went down to the restaurant for breakfast and had barely sat down before a shadow crossed her table.

"Mind if I join you?"

She looked up and stared at the most handsome man she had ever seen.

"Lucas, what are you doing here?" she said, surprised yet happy to see him.

"I believe the same thing you are," he grinned, sitting.

She flushed at her stupidity. Of course he was here for Izzy and Marco's engagement party.

"I didn't expect to see you until tonight," she said, remembering he hadn't been with Tonio last night when they arrived.

Lucas and Tonio both planned to meet the women at the hotel and hopefully spend the night having hot and spectacular sex with their respective partners. Unfortunately Lucas got caught up at work and couldn't leave with Tonio, making him catch a much later flight. It didn't matter he had only a few hours sleep because knowing he was seeing Montana again energised him.

"I understand that you're sightseeing today and thought I could offer my services," he said.

"Oh, you don't have to do that, I'm sure that you're probably too busy to do such boring things like look at churches and museums."

"Do you not want to spend time with me?" The question came out a little more abrupt than he planned. He meant to tease her into accepting his company, but after remembering how she left after Marco's birthday without even leaving a phone number, he wondered if she didn't feel the same attraction towards him as he did to her.

A twinge of guilt slithered through her knowing she was still torn over her feelings for Lucas. Yes, she was attracted to him but what future was there for them? She wasn't the type of woman to just use a man and she definitely wasn't willing to get her heart broken again. Once was enough.

What made her feel even guiltier was the fact she knew, and was still trying hard to deny, her extremely strong feelings for Lucas and she could easily fall in love with him in the blink of an eye. Again, she strongly squashed down that voice inside her which said she already had.

"Of course I do, it's just that I thought someone as busy as you just wouldn't have time for something so frivolous, especially since I'm only sightseeing," she said, not wanting him to feel like he had to step in like she was his obligation.

"It's a Saturday so it's the weekend and I'm free."

She smiled and it hit him like a punch to the stomach.

"In that case, I'd love to spend the day with you," she said.

And hopefully all night, he thought but squashed down any thoughts about getting too far ahead of himself since this was Montana and so he shouldn't count his chickens too soon.

They spent a glorious morning together, laughing and chatting. Montana was excited and in awe of nearly everything they saw.

Finally they decided to take a break and have a late lunch.

"This has been so wonderful, hasn't it?" she beamed. "There's just so much history here and things I never even knew about."

Lucas couldn't help but smile at Montana's enthusiasm. If he was being honest, he thought she would have given up after an hour and decide to either shop or go back to the hotel. Instead they walked for miles, more than he had in ages and she was only starting to tire now.

"So how's the Ferrari?" she said, remembering Marco's birthday.

The question took him by surprise. He hadn't expected Montana to ask him about his car.

"Actually I decided to sell it."

"What? Why? You said you loved that car." The surprised look on her face made him want to kiss her.

"I did for about two seconds and then realised that it just wasn't what I wanted."

He looked solemn which hooked her curiosity.

"So what did you buy instead?"

"A Lamborgini," he grinned.

She almost threw her bread roll at him as she laughed.

"Oh you…"

"Gotcha."

"Well, I'll be looking forward to test driving it when I go to Italy."

"I'll have sold it by then," he quickly said.

"It doesn't matter, I'm sure whatever sports car you have will be fine," she teased.

"In that case, I'm getting a big bus," he chuckled.

After lunch they went back to the hotel and just as Montana was torn between inviting him up to her room or not, a feminine voice rang out.

"Lucas *darling*, what fantastic timing."

Lucas turned, saw the woman calling out to him and stifled a groan. Patrizia Rossi was not only one of Marco's sisters' best friends, but he stupidly slept with her once years ago. Right now she was someone he didn't want to see.

"Patrizia, what a surprise," he said, gritting his teeth as she threw himself at him.

"I know, isn't it," she purred. "I'm here for Marco's engagement party of course, just like you. I'm so glad I managed to run into you, I haven't seen you in ages. And what luck we're staying at the same hotel."

It wasn't hard to know the family would be staying in this hotel since the Romero family not only owned one of the largest Italian food manufacturing companies but also a chain of hotels and many other various businesses.

Before he could tell Patrizia he was busy, he turned and found Montana had disappeared. Stifling a sigh knowing there was now no way that he was going to see her before Marco's engagement party, he knew he wasn't about to spend any time with Patrizia either.

"Sorry, Patrizia, I have to get going. My father wants me to call him," he lied.

"Of course. We can catch up tonight, it'll be the perfect chance to *reconnect*," she purred.

At that moment he knew he'd be avoiding her as much as possible.

"Sure," he said, walking away without a backwards glance.

Montana might not know who the classy woman who knew Lucas downstairs was, but she was smart enough to know the woman was interested in him, judging by the way her whole face lit up upon seeing him, not to mention the desire in her eyes.

Lying down on her bed, she thought to close her eyes for just a few minutes, but then heard a loud and persistent ringing that wouldn't stop. Her eyelids were heavy and it took a while to realise she had fallen into a deep sleep.

"Hello?" she mumbled, still trying to wake up.

"Thank goodness," Toni said. "I've been trying to get a hold of you for ages."

"Sorry, I fell asleep. I must have been more tired than I thought."

"Well, get your glad rags on, we have an engagement party to get to."

Looking at the clock, she got a fright at the time.

"Oh gosh, what time do we have to leave?"

"In half an hour. That's why I was ringing, to see if you were okay since I hadn't heard from you all day."

"I'll be as quick as I can."

She hung up and started rushing around. Her shower might have been the fastest on record, but it was drying of her hair that was taking the longest time, making her flustered and panicked.

A knock sounded at her door.

Quickly she went to open it, relieved to see Toni.

"I'm not ready," she said. "My hair is taking ages."

"Its okay, breathe," Toni said. "I warned Tonio you were running late and he said it'll be fine since it's a party with finger food and not a sit down meal."

"Thank goodness," she said, relieved.

Finally getting her hair sorted, she did her make-up while chatting away to her best friend.

"So do I ask what time you two got out of bed?" She raised a curious eyebrow.

"About half an hour before I rang you," Toni flushed.

"Well, you look stunning," she laughed. "Thanks for the wake-up call. I can't believe how tired I was. Must have just been all that sightseeing and sun."

"How was Lucas?" Toni grinned.

Her mouth fell open in surprise.

"You know Lucas came sightseeing with me?"

"How do you think he knew to? Tonio let him know that I was *unavailable*," Toni said, beet red.

"Well, it was great. You missed some wonderful things."

"Oh, I don't know, I saw some pretty wonderful things myself."

They both burst into laughter and then there was a knock at the door.

"Oh, that'll be Tonio and Lucas."

Montana felt her nerves humming and took a few quick deep breaths.

"Good thing I'm ready, let's go celebrate."

Seeing the two Romero cousins on the other side of the door in tuxedos blew Montana away. She didn't think she had ever seen such handsome men before.

"You look stunning," Lucas said. "Good sleep?"

"Yes," she flushed. "I didn't realise how tired I was until Toni called and woke me up."

She didn't ask who the woman was downstairs or if Lucas spent any time with her. It was none of her business, but still she felt uncomfortable.

Chapter Twelve

The party was lively and Izzy and Marco were delighted to see their friends and cousins arrive.

"I'm so glad that you came," Izzy said, hugging her best friends.

"So are we. The place looks fantastic," she said.

"Toni and Tonio seem to have made up for lost time," Izzy grinned, seeing the couple so close.

"I believe that their reunion celebration only ended about an hour or so ago because we had an engagement party to attend," she giggled.

"Wow. Perhaps I need to have words with Marco. Clearly now we're engaged, he's letting the romance die," Izzy teased. "What about you and Lucas?"

"We spent most of the day sightseeing."

"That's all?" Izzy arched an eyebrow.

"That's all." She wasn't about to dwell on Lucas or the

woman from the hotel. Tonight she was going to socialise and catch up with the people she hadn't seen in years. "Now where are your parents, I can't wait to see them."

"Mamá's in the crimson sequin gown delighting in the fact I'm finally getting married. Don't be surprised if you keep hearing her repeat how wonderful it is and how long I made her wait." Izzy rolled her eyes.

"Well, it is great and I'm so happy for you."

Montana found Izzy's mother and received a bone-crushing hug.

"Montana, we're so excited to have you here. It's been years. I can't believe Bella is finally getting married," Consuela Esteban said, unable to hide her excitement.

"It's fantastic and Marco's a wonderful guy."

"Sí. It would have been nicer for her to marry a nice *Spanish* man but I'll take what I can get since she's getting on and I want grandchildren before I die."

If Izzy could hear her mother, Montana knew there would be a lot of eye rolling happening.

"She's not *that* old," she laughed.

Consuela huffed and before she could reply, Rosa Esteban, Izzy's grandmother, joined them.

"Mamá, this is Montana, one of Bella's friends from New Zealand," Consuela said.

"Hola, its lovely to meet you. I'm sorry but I don't speak any Spanish," Montana said. "I hope you're feeling better."

"Sí, thank you for asking. Bella's engagement is just what the doctor ordered. Now I have the will to live to see my great-grandchildren being born."

Montana stifled another chuckle and eye roll on Izzy's behalf. After knowing Izzy all these years, she knew just how melodramatic Izzy and her family were. She stayed and chatted to Rosa for a while before she saw Toni waving to her.

"Please excuse me, I see my friend waving to me," she said.

"Go enjoy yourself. Thank you for keeping an old woman company for a few minutes," Rosa said, waving her away.

"How are you enjoying the party so far?" Montana said, joining Toni and Tonio.

"Its fantastic, the food has been delicious and everyone seems friendly and lovely," Toni said, then lowered her voice to whisper in Montana's ear. "Although I have to say Marco's sisters aren't the friendliest of people."

"Oh?"

"No, they seem a bit snobby."

"I haven't met them yet. Which ones are they?"

Toni discreetly pointed out Marco's sisters who seemed to be standing in a group together with their partners.

"Are they all married?"

"The elder two are but the youngest isn't, although she does have a boyfriend, the tall guy wearing glasses."

"Perhaps I'll meet them later," she said, making a mental note to make it much later if what Toni said was true. She hadn't seen them at Marco's birthday party but then, she hadn't really been paying attention to any of the guests and wasn't even sure if they attended or not.

All night Lucas kept subtle tabs on Montana, making sure he didn't crowd her since he knew she wanted to catch up with Isabella's family. He was also enjoying chatting and mingling with his own extended family who came to help celebrate even though they were doing it all again in a few weeks in Italy.

Seeing Montana now talking to Toni, he saw his chance to reconnect with her but as he moved towards their group, Patrizia stepped into his path.

"You look as handsome and *sexy* as ever," she purred, her hand reaching up to brush his shoulder and then move down to his chest. "It's a shame we didn't manage to catch up today, perhaps we can privately later tonight?"

He knew what Patrizia wanted, and so he removed her arm and proceeded to ignore her, but she once again stepped in front of him with a sultry pout.

"Aren't you going to say how hot and sexy I look? I think this dress shows off my figure quite nicely, don't you?"

"It's never going to happen. Now if you'll excuse me."

His face was like granite, not teasing or playing hard to get, nor did his eyes move from looking over her shoulder. Patrizia wanted to stomp her feet but instead, gracefully moved to one side to let him past and as she watched who now had Lucas' attention, she was fuming. Lucas was meant to be hers, not some nobody from some far flung country no one cared about.

"Are you enjoying yourself?" he said, putting his arm around Montana's shoulders, happy she didn't move away.

"Of course. Its great to see Izzy and Marco so happy and in love. Not to mention seeing her parents again," she said.

"Dance with me," he said, taking her hand and giving it a kiss.

Her stomach somersaulted and before she could answer, he was leading her to the dance floor.

"Finally I have you in my arms again. Unfortunately we're not alone."

She smiled enjoying being in Lucas' arms as well. They had never danced together before and she couldn't help but notice how well they fitted.

"Do you realise that this is our first dance together?"

"The first of many, I hope," he said and then to her surprise, twirled her.

"You're going to make me dizzy if you keep doing that," she laughed.

"Will it make you lose your senses and end up in my bed?"

The heat from his eyes made her blush and she couldn't deny she was tempted. Could she do another one-night stand with Lucas? Did she want to? Oh yes, she did!

"I'm not sure that's a good idea," she said, unable to look him in the eye because then he'd know just how much she really wanted to.

"Why not?" He sounded indignant.

"Because we can't just keep going around sleeping with each other every time we see each other."

"I think it's a great idea. You know we're spectacular together."

Silently she agreed and her willpower was fading fast so she took a deep breath.

"I'm not the type of woman to just be someone's bed buddy. You don't get to just use me to scratch your itch, Lucas."

"Well, I don't mind if you use me to scratch yours," he grinned and she couldn't help but laugh and then sobered.

"I mean it."

"What if I think of you as more than an itch to scratch?"

In the middle of the dance floor wasn't really the place to have this type of conversation and yet, Montana felt relaxed and so she was willing to continue on and make him see sense.

Although the heat in his eyes and the huskiness in his voice made her legs feel like jelly, it was lucky he was holding her close. Unfortunately now she could feel his arousal and it was just making it worse as she was also becoming aroused herself.

"We live in two different countries and hardly see each other. It would be all kinds of awkward to travel down this path — not just for us but our friends and family too."

"Well, I have to say, you living in London is a lot easier to get to than New Zealand, however, I can see your point *but* it doesn't mean it couldn't work. I'll fly over often and you can come to Italy."

"But that's my point. I want to see more of Europe, travel, do and see all those things tourists do. I can't do all that and keep seeing you, I'm not made of money."

"Then I'll come and travel with you."

She loved he was so optimistic and could easily bat away all her worries, but unfortunately she also knew words weren't reality. Sighing, she closed her eyes and pulled him tighter, laying her head on his shoulder, letting the music flow over her so she could just enjoy the moment of being in Lucas' arms.

Finally the music ended and slowly he released her.

"Will you at least think about it?" he said.

"Yes, but don't get your hopes up."

"Then tell me what it would take for us to be more than bed buddies."

"I really don't know," she sighed.

He led her off the dance floor and went to get them a drink. Montana took the chance to go to the restroom for some breathing space.

Maybe it was being in Spain or Europe. Maybe it was seeing Lucas again, which was making her unsure what this all meant. What she did know was she still had strong feelings for him and they hadn't gone away as much as she thought.

Maybe she could enjoy the night with him, but wasn't that just a repeat of San Miguel, something she told him she didn't want? Annoyed at her own contrariness, and still none the wiser about what to do about Lucas, she silently prayed she'd be able to work it out by the time the evening ended.

On the way back to find him, she was waylaid by three women who, thanks to Toni's earlier observation, Montana knew to be Marco's sisters and the woman from the hotel this afternoon. From the looks on their faces, she felt a strange sinking sensation. What were they all about?

"Are you Lucas' girlfriend?" Pia, Marco's eldest sister said.

"Oh, I —" She was caught off guard by the question and their abruptness. "I'm sorry, who are you?"

"We're Marco's sisters, Pia and Allegra. This is our best friend, Patrizia Rossi," Pia said.

"So are you?" Allegra said.

The unexpected confrontation made Montana feel like she was in an interrogation and anxiety flooded through her.

"I don't think that —"

"Look, the only reason we're asking is because he's *our cousin* and well, a playboy. We'd hate to see you get caught up in some sort of silly romantic notion he's serious about you when all he wants to do is sleep with you," Pia said.

"Then dump you," Allegra said.

"Thank you for the warning, I'll take it into consideration," she said as politely as possible, getting her breathing under control so she was calm once again. These women were acting like bitchy teenagers and she really wanted to tell them to mind their own business.

"We're trying to help you," Patrizia said, trying to sound sympathetic. "I think you should know that Lucas and I have an *understanding*."

"An understanding?" she said, puzzled as all three women's heads nodded their agreement.

"Yes, its an understanding between us and our families that we'll be married," Patrizia said. Once again, Pia and

Allegra nodded their agreement. "So you see, he's only using you."

"So you're engaged?" Montana said, clarifying the situation.

"Not yet, but it's only a matter of time," Allegra said.

"So Lucas is free to play the field until he becomes engaged…to *you*…"

"That's right," Patrizia beamed. "I'm so glad that you understand."

"Perfectly," she smiled. "You've just made my decision so much simpler. Grazie."

She walked off silently laughing to herself. Did Marco's sisters and their friend really think they were warning Montana off Lucas with their insincere caring routine. She knew what jealousy looked like and Patrizia had it in spades. Clearly, Patrizia never noticed Montana with Lucas this afternoon at the hotel but if she had, was that what brought out the green-eyed jealousy monster?

Even if what Patrizia said was true, did the silly woman really think she wouldn't ask Lucas about it? She wasn't brought up with subterfuge. In her family it was always best to get the answer you wanted from the horse's mouth, that way there could be no misunderstandings or people able to manipulate the situation. This type of blunt honesty was required in a family of six siblings as it cleared the air and stopped a lot of fights before they happened.

She returned to her friends who were laughing and talking.

"I saw you talking to Marco's sisters," Izzy said, curious.

"Oh yes." She paused, wanting to make sure that she had *everyone's* attention. "They told me that Lucas and Patrizia had an *understanding* and that he's free to play the field until they get engaged."

The bombshell was dropped and she couldn't help but giggle at her friends' reactions.

"They what?" Lucas said, gobsmacked.

"What understanding?" Marco said, confused.

"Ooh, someone's jealous," Izzy grinned.

"Is there something you want to tell us, Luc?" Tonio teased.

"I can't believe my sisters would say something like that, are you sure?" Marco said.

Izzy, sensing her fiancé's anger was simmering, squeezed his hand holding him closer to try and calm him down.

"Definitely," Montana grinned. "It was a very enlightening conversation about wanting to protect me from any romantic notions I might have about Lucas."

Lucas stood there still speechless that his own cousins would not only say something like that, but make up untruths and meddle in his private life.

"I don't understand why you're telling us?" Marco said, puzzled.

"Your sisters and their friend thought I'd be so upset and too embarrassed to mention it, but when you come from a family like mine, *misunderstandings* occur all the time with people trying to manipulate and either pull a sneaky or cause trouble," she said. "It's better to just get it out there to clear the air, make sure what's been said is true. Believe me, you have no idea how many times people have tried to play us siblings off against each other. It never works."

"I'll have a word with my sisters," Marco said, visibly angry now.

"Please don't. Just act like you don't know anything, that way if they try to create any more mischief, we'll all know that's all it is," Montana said. "Besides, the best way to get them back is for Lucas and I to leave together. It'll drive them nuts."

The Romero cousins were astounded by Montana's reaction as Izzy and Toni smiled.

"I still don't understand," Marco said, shaking his head.

"When it comes to psychological warfare, I'm an expert. Just spend some time with my siblings and you'll get it," Montana grinned. "Now, if it won't upset the engaged couple, I propose Lucas takes me back to the hotel."

"Oh, can we go too?" Toni said, looking to Izzy for her permission. She was dying to be alone with Tonio once again.

"Sure, but don't forget we have lunch tomorrow," Izzy scowled and then smiled. "I want *all* the sexy details."

"We'll see," Montana grinned.

Lucas couldn't believe his luck. He didn't think Montana was going to sleep with him again, but his cousins and Patrizia clearly goaded her and he was silently thankful.

"What exactly did my cousins and Patrizia say to you? I mean, earlier you weren't that keen to just be a bed buddy?

You don't have to do this, I'm happy to just pretend and annoy the heck out of them," he said, lying through his teeth. He wanted Montana in bed, there was no doubt about that.

"Apparently you're a free agent until you get engaged."

"And that turns you on?" he said, confused.

"No, but the thought that I could be the last woman you sleep with before you get tied down appealed."

She wasn't about to admit she felt a certain amount of possessiveness over Lucas, which she hadn't realised until Patrizia and Marco's sisters tried to scare her away.

Well, one thing was for certain, she had subconsciously been looking for a sign to tell her whether sleeping with Lucas again was a good idea, and she just received it in blinking neon green lights. This was also a good excuse to lie to herself about why she was going to sleep with him again.

"Now I get it. That old competitive streak."

"That's the one. The one where you might be marrying her, but in bed you'll only be thinking of me and how hot it was and how you'll never get it again," she teased.

"I guess I better make sure that I drag out my freedom for as long as possible."

"Or if this is your last night of freedom, we make sure that we have as much sex and in every position possible."

"I like your thinking."

That was the last thing either of them said for the rest of the night.

Chapter Thirteen

The next morning just before the three couples were due to meet up for lunch there was a flurry of texting and calling before all parties agreed lunch was out and they should instead meet up late afternoon.

It seemed everyone was in the same mind, no one wanted to get out of bed.

Now the three women sat on the beach far enough away from the men so they could talk privately although everyone knew all the gossip would be eventually swapped.

"So, since you came with Lucas I assume that you two spent the night together?" Izzy said, eager for news.

"I'll be honest. I wasn't going to," she said. "I don't want to just be his bed buddy every time we meet but..."

"*But...*" Toni said.

"Well, that run in with Marco's sisters and their friend just made me mad. And possibly made me realise that I like him a lot so…"

"*So…*" Izzy said.

"Stop making us drag this out of you," Toni growled.

"So, I thought, why can't I just be one of those women who enjoys a fling."

The look on her two best friends faces made her feel deflated. She knew exactly what they were thinking, they had known each other too long.

"Mon, I'm sorry. As happy as I am that you like Lucas, you're not a *fling* kind of girl," Izzy said, as gently as possible.

"I agree. Mon, you like him *a lot*. We all know it, but we also all know how scared you are. Have you told him about James?" Toni said.

"I can't." She shook her head. "Like I said, we're not in a relationship. To be honest we don't really do much deep and meaningful stuff. We hardly know each other except in bed," she said, miserable.

"Then I say, just use him and let the chips fall where they may," Izzy said, supportive.

"Why can't you have a superficial sex only *fling* with a hot guy." Toni added her agreement.

Montana loved having such supportive friends and had no idea what she would have done without them.

Joining up with the men, it was Marco who said, "So we'll be seeing you all in Italy for round two, right?"

"Yes, Marco and I leave first thing in the morning, when are you guys leaving Spain?" Izzy said.

"Well, I only managed to get an extra day so I leave tomorrow night," Toni said.

"And I got two days, so early evening the night after that," Montana said.

"So what do you have planned for your remaining days?" Marco said.

"Well, *we* were *supposed* to be sightseeing, me more so since I've never been to Spain before, but it seems even the best laid plans…" Montana teased.

Toni flushed as Tonio chuckled and gathered his girlfriend to him. It was unspoken that they were back together and once again in a relationship.

To Lucas it seemed like this was San Miguel all over again and knowing Montana was remaining in Spain for a few extra days was an opportunity not to be missed. Before he could tee it up with his father, Marco surprised him.

"That's great because Lucas has to stay for a few days for work. Perhaps you could keep each other company."

"He does?" Tonio said, confused. Marco glared at his cousin, but everyone noted his faux pas. "Oops, I mean, yes he does."

"Nice try," Montana said, as everyone laughed. She couldn't believe everyone was trying to set her and Lucas up again, but this time she had to admit, she didn't mind it. "I'm happy with or without company."

"Great, then we can sightsee together. I have to admit, I haven't seen much of this area."

"Well as long as you're not going to get into trouble," Montana worried.

"He won't," Marco said, confident.

"I should probably call my father and let him know about the change in plans."

"We're going to go and find a restaurant for dinner, want to come or wait for Lucas?" Izzy said.

"I'll wait."

Lucas called his father, who hadn't come to the engagement party because he hurt his back playing tennis earlier that week. His mother also hadn't attended as his eldest sister was due to give birth any day and she wasn't about to miss the birth of her first grandchild. Only his sisters, Sofia and Paola travelled to Spain however, they ended up missing most of the party and not arriving until well after Montana and Lucas had already departed. Their first setback was due to Giana being in labour, which turned out to be a false alarm, and then there was an issue with the plane causing the next delay. According to Marco, by the time Sofia and Paola arrived at the party, his sisters were very upset about their late arrival.

Montana walked down to the water's edge and looked out at the beauty of the ocean.

Two women and a dog were walking on the beach and she smiled seeing the dog enjoying frolicking in the water until it shook out its coat right beside her.

"Aah" She squealed in fright. "Thank you for sharing with me, but I was fine just getting my feet wet." She smiled at the little dog as she bent down to pat it.

"Oh, I'm so sorry, are you okay?" one of the women said, before looking at her dog. "You naughty dog."

"It's okay, its only water. Are you a tourist like me?"

"Sort of. My friend and I are catching up. This is her dog we're walking. What about you?"

"I'm just here for a friend's engagement party."

"Oh, how wonderful. Your accent isn't European, where are you from?"

"New Zealand."

"That's a long way to travel for an engagement party."

"I'm currently living in London," she laughed. "Otherwise, I wouldn't be here. Where are you from?"

"Italy."

"I've never been there, but my friend is having another engagement party in Italy so I'm also going to that."

"Oh, you'll love it. There's so much history and amazing things to see and do. Not to mention all the Italian men to ogle."

Montana laughed and wanted to say she already had her own Italian man to ogle, but didn't.

"I'll make sure that's on my list of things to do in Italy — ogle hunky Italian men."

"Well, I'd better catch up with my friend."

As Montana looked around, she noted the dog and the other woman were now further down the beach.

"It was nice to meet you," Montana said.

"You too," the lady said, walking off.

Turning to walk back to Lucas who was just finishing his call, she smiled. Yes, he definitely was an Italian hunk worth ogling, especially naked.

"Who were you talking too?" he said, curious. He

couldn't be certain but the woman looked an awfully lot like his younger sister, Sofia.

"Just a person I met on the beach. Her friend's dog shook water all over me."

"So she didn't give you a name?"

She looked at him oddly.

"No, we just chatted. She was Italian and said that I should make sure when I go, to ogle some Italian hunks."

His face turned into a scowl. Now that sounded like Sofia.

"You won't have time for that."

"To ogle hunks, I'll make time, tons of it," she teased.

He swept her leg so they both fell onto the sand with him on top and he stared into her brown eyes.

"I'm the only Italian hunk you get to ogle, got that."

"Is that some kind of threat," she said, her breathing jagged, as she felt his arousal and she wanted him to kiss her.

"Not a threat, a promise."

"Will you be naked?" she teased.

His eyes flared with desire as his face got closer so there was only a whisper of breath between them.

"Only for you," he said, before thoroughly kissing her.

The only thing that managed to interrupt their very scorching kiss was the fact Lucas' phone was ringing.

"Your phone," she said, breathless.

"Ignore it," he said, capturing her lips again but the insistent ringtone meant it was his cousin.

They sat up with matching silly smiles and as Lucas answered the phone, Montana saw the woman she talked to give her a wave and smile.

Embarrassed the woman saw her kissing Lucas made Montana duck her head into his chest.

"They've found a restaurant and are waiting for us," he said, pocketing his phone.

After dinner and saying goodbye to Marco and Izzy with promises they'd see them in Italy, Toni told Montana she'd see her back in London in a few days as she went off with Tonio leaving Lucas and Montana all alone.

"Finally, no more catch ups and interruptions," he grinned.

"But we do have to plan what sights we're going to see."

"Can't we just spend the next two days in bed?"

"You can," she smiled. "But I'm here to see the sights. Who knows when I'll be back, if ever."

"But it's all churches and museums," he groaned.

"No, its not. There tons of things we can do, see." She opened up her travel map showing all the tourist attractions and while Lucas was correct that there were a lot of churches dotted around the city, there were tons of other things from historical walks to wine tastings and one that was her personal favourite, a dessert shop that sold the most unique flavours of gelato and ice cream and what looked like the most delicious desserts. Now that sounded like heaven to her and with a name like Gelato Heaven, she was sure it would be. Taking the map away, he led her to the bed and began taking his own exploratory adventure.

Once again Montana and Lucas spent all morning sightseeing before a late lunch.

"Since I've done so much walking, I feel like I deserve a reward," she said.

Lucas' eyes smouldered in total agreement, already picturing his reward.

"I totally agree. Let's go back to the hotel."

"What for?"

"My reward," he grinned.

Montana felt herself react to his words. She too, wanted that but first…

"This blood orange flavour is heaven," she sighed.

"You've said that about the last fifty you've tasted," he smiled, wondering what she would think if he tried licking that off her body especially in an area which he considered to be heaven.

After dragging him to Gelato Heaven, Montana ordered the All You Can Eat menu where diners could have a taste of any of the desserts or gelatos on offer. They came in small tasting sizes so that diners could sample more or reorder the same thing but bigger if they liked it that much. They also got to take home a tub of their choice as well.

Since she started tasting, all she did was constantly lick her lips, sigh at how wonderful it tasted and then repeat for the next one.

Lucas may not have been impressed she vetoed returning to the hotel to come to Gelato Heaven, however, watching Montana's face as she ate as many flavours of gelato as possible was highly erotic and even the coldness of the product couldn't stop his arousal from growing.

"And it would be all true. Thank goodness I don't live here, I'd practically live in this place."

"You're only loving it because it's a novelty."

"That's true but still, I love ice cream and would probably be their best customer," she grinned. "Do you think they have other stores in Europe?"

He could see Montana making her own tour of Europe based on where the stores were located and it made him smile.

"I hope not, you'd never see anything of Europe's history otherwise," he chuckled.

"It would be a lot more fun than all the churches and cathedrals."

"That's true, but wouldn't eating at one be like eating at them all?"

"I'm sure that they'd have only exclusive flavours for that store."

"Sounds like you've really thought this all out."

"Sure have," she grinned. "Now let's see, what do I want to taste next."

By the time Montana finally declared herself full, she practically skipped back to the hotel with excitement that Gelato Heaven did indeed have two more stores — one in Italy and one in France. Currently they didn't have one in London to her disappointment.

"I believe it's now my turn for dessert." he said, once they were inside her room.

The hunger in his eyes made her quiver in anticipation and before she knew it they were both naked and Lucas miraculously produce a small tub of gelato.

"How did you…?"

"I have my ways," he grinned. "Now let's see if this really tastes like heaven."

Later on as they both lay there breathless, he said, "Definitely heaven."

"I saw the stars and have to agree."

Montana couldn't get over how right it felt spending time with Lucas. If only they lived in the same country they could try and make a go of it. Unfortunately they didn't, and their idyllic few days were almost at an end.

"I don't want to go back to reality," she said, tightly hugging him after yet another magical sex session.

He kissed the top of her head and held her closer to him.

"Me either but we'll see each other soon."

"And then what? This is why I didn't just want to be a bed buddy. I knew this was going to get difficult," Montana said.

"Hey, we can work something out. Being together these past few days, surely shows how right we are together."

"But we don't live in the same country."

"We can make this work, Mon. I mean it."

His words were the reassurance she needed to hear but still she was anxious this was all going to turn into a disaster.

"Perhaps we can find you a job in Italy?" he said.

"But I don't speak Italian," she said, miserable.

"I'll hire you a tutor."

"A hunky Italian one will make me learn faster," she teased.

He growled and rolled on top of her, staring deeply into her eyes, reminding Montana of the moment she met him on the beach in San Miguel — their connection.

"No way. The only hunky Italian tutor you get is me. I'll hire you a female so you'll concentrate and not be distracted."

"I guess there are a few words you could teach me," she said, pulling him down to whisper into his ear.

Once more they lay panting with silly smiles on their faces.

"I think I may need a few more lessons," she said.

"Here's how you say, ride me, ride me hard," he said, pulling her on top of him.

Saying goodbye to Lucas at the airport, even though she would be seeing him in a few weeks, was still upsetting and she couldn't help but cry all the way back to London.

To her surprise when she returned to the flat she shared with Toni, Tonio was in residence.

"I hope you don't mind that he came back with me for the next few weeks," Toni said, sheepish.

"Of course not," she said, wishing Lucas had done the same romantic thing even if she still wasn't sure about them as a couple. "I'm glad to see that you two seem to have worked it out."

"Actually Mon, Tonio wants me to see if perhaps I could either move to Italy or he'll try to get himself moved to London. Would you be okay with that?"

Montana would miss her best friend terribly if Toni moved to Italy and she was left here all by herself, but seeing the hope on Toni's face, she knew she needed to be supportive.

"Of course I will be," she said, putting on a brave uncertain face.

The days dragged on and not just because Lucas was constantly in her thoughts and rang nearly every day, but because she also lost her job, which although wasn't a big loss, just meant added stress to try and find a new one.

Luckily it was Tonio who managed to find her a temporary job at a top hotel in their laundry department. Montana didn't mind at all since the pay was fantastic and the job was finishing up just before she was due to leave for Italy.

Lucas rang to see how her first day on the job went.

"So how did it go?"

"Its hard work, but I just keep reminding myself that its only temporary and the pay is way more than I would have made in months at my old job so I'll suck it up," she said, exhausted but happy.

Lucas didn't tell her he had Tonio arrange the job at higher pay than normal since this was their hotel.

"I have an idea," he said.

"What's that?"

"Since your temping job is up before you come, why don't you stay for a few weeks?"

"Oh, I don't know," she said, hesitant. "I really need to get back and find another job since I'll be unemployed and don't know how long it will take me to find another one."

"Please Mon. I miss you. I'll pay for your expenses while you're here."

"I'll think about it." She desperately wanted to say yes, but still wasn't confident whether she and Lucas had a future or not.

Sensing Montana's reluctance, he decided to change the topic to something a lot happier.

"Guess what?" he said.

"What?" She could sense his smiling down the line.

"My sister's finally had her baby."

"No way! That's fantastic. Congratulations. What is it, a boy or girl? Does it have a name yet? Your parents must be over the moon."

He enjoyed hearing the excitement in her voice and wished she were with him to help celebrate.

"The poor thing keeps being handed around like a sack of potatoes. Everyone wants to hold her but she is cute. I'll send you a photo."

"How's your sister doing? Is she okay?"

It warmed him that Montana cared to ask about Giana.

"She's fine but tired. Oh, and the baby's name is Petra."

"Oh, that's so pretty. Does Tonio know yet?"

"Probably, I think my mother has told all of Italy she's got her first grandchild," he chuckled. "It's also probably not at the top of Tonio's list of things to tell you so don't be surprised if you tell him about the baby and he's the one that looks surprised."

As predicted, Tonio did indeed look surprised Montana knew about Giana's baby before him.

"Lucas said that you'd probably be surprised," she giggled.

He looked at his phone and went sheepish.

"It seems I did get a message about it."

Both Toni and Montana laughed as he held up the phone to show them the pictures of Petra which both women gushed over.

Chapter Fourteen

They were excitedly winging their way to Italy and thanks to Tonio, they were going in style — the Romero family corporate jet.

"Wow, this is luxury," she said, rubbing the soft leather of her seat.

"It's definitely the only way to travel," Toni giggled.

"It feels a little weird not having all these other passengers surrounding you."

"It's great, isn't it?"

Tonio just sat there smiling at the two women. To him, this was normal but he enjoyed how wonderful they thought it. Then he wondered how Montana was going to react when she found out she was staying with Lucas and not in a hotel as planned.

"I can't wait to see the hotel, its supposed to be in the heart of the city and the best part is I can sleep in, just roll out of bed and then I'll be able to walk everywhere to see all the sights," Montana said.

Neither woman noticed Tonio's frown and thoughtful look.

"I need to make a quick phone call," he said, leaving them to go into the little bedroom.

"Well, that was weird," she said.

"Totally," Toni said, wondering what Tonio was really doing.

Tonio quickly called Lucas.

"You'd better get her hotel room back," he panicked.

"Why?"

"Because if she finds out you've cancelled it and are having her stay with you, she's going to be very angry *with you*."

"No, she won't. It'll be great."

"I don't think you understand, Luc. She just said how much she's looking forward to being at the hotel — the fact she can walk to all the sights, sleep in, all that stuff. I hate to say it but not once did she mention *you*." He hoped he was stressing the urgency to his cousin.

"Really? Didn't mention me at all?" Lucas sounded hurt.

"Look, just get her room back and I say let her decide otherwise she'll be furious. If she chooses to stay with you, great. Otherwise, just let her do her thing. After all, don't forget you are still working."

Tonio made some very valid points, Lucas thought. He did have a few things needing his attention and couldn't take too much time off to spend his days with Montana, no matter how much he wanted to.

After returning from Spain, he grilled his sister, Sofia to see if she was indeed the woman on the beach who Montana talked to. Although Sofia tried to feign innocence, under Lucas' penetrating gaze, she confessed.

"I only wanted to meet her to see for myself what she was like since Pia and Allegra made cutting remarks about her," she said. "Of course that brief encounter wasn't long enough to know, but she seems really nice."

Sofia had heard plenty of disparaging comments from her cousins, Pia and Allegra and their friend, Patrizia at lunch the next day. Her cousins also moaned about Marco scolding them for saying Lucas and Patrizia had some sort of understanding. They didn't know how he knew and tried to tell him that clearly *that* woman was mischief making against his own sisters.

Sofia wasn't stupid. Lucas may or may not be dating the woman her cousins disliked, but there was definitely no way her brother was ever going to have any kind of understanding with someone like Patrizia Rossi. She knew Patrizia well enough to know that while Patrizia might have set her sights on Lucas, like most women she knew, the fact Patrizia and Sofia's cousins were manipulating and lying showed Patrizia didn't have feelings for Lucas. She was just after his money and that made Sofia angry.

She could only cross her fingers and hope Lucas wouldn't fall for such manipulative tricks, as did their elder sister Paola, who like Sofia, hadn't met the woman their cousins were moaning about. Lucas' two sisters, decided they too would be watching Montana with eagle eyes to see if she was playing some kind of game with their brother. The last thing either of them wanted was a manipulative future sister-in-law they not only couldn't stand, but who made their brother's life a misery.

Seeing Montana and Lucas together with her own two eyes, unaware Sofia was watching, helped reassure Sofia that the couple did indeed look enamoured with each other, that it wasn't just one way.

"I'll admit I did see you together on the beach and thought you both looked happy and carefree, like a real couple in love," she said.

Lucas exhaled a loud breath at his younger sister's explanation and then silently cursed his cousins.

"Then you'll at least give Montana a chance and ignore Pia and Allegra's bias. They just want me to end up with Patrizia," he said, ignoring the fact his sister thought they looked *in love*. It wasn't love, it was just lust.

Never before had he needed to explain his romantic liaisons to his sisters, but Montana was different and seeing Sofia screw up her face at the mention of Patrizia, relaxed him.

"I suggest you introduce her to *us* as soon as possible, that way even if everyone's heard their comments, they can see for themselves that Montana's not what they've heard...hopefully," she said. "It could also be a good diversion for Giana since she's exhausted with all the visitors and mamma smothering her and the baby."

"I'm assuming Paola also heard the comments?" He arched an eyebrow.

"Sì, she was there when they were complaining."

"So she thinks Montana is also all wrong for me?" He couldn't believe the mischief his cousins were causing.

"We both agreed to give Montana a chance, that's why you really need to introduce us as soon as possible," she said, feeling sorry for her brother.

"When I see her, I'll see if she's up for a family lunch," he sighed.

Sofia smiled. She really hadn't thought Lucas would listen to her suggestion but the fact he had, meant he must like Montana *a lot*. She needed to talk to Paola and see how they could subtly interrogate Montana without her realising. After all, Lucas was her brother and she wanted to make sure Montana was the right woman for him.

It was dark when they landed and as they stepped off the plane Montana was surprised to see Lucas waiting for her. Her heart accelerated upon seeing him again and she couldn't deny she had missed him even for those few weeks apart. His constant calls weren't the same thing as seeing him in person.

"What are you doing here?" she smiled.

"Welcoming you to Italy of course," he said, kissing her with a thoroughness that left her breathless and without any doubt he also missed her.

"Wow," she panted. "I'm loving Italy already."

"I have an offer for you," he said, hesitant. "I can either take you to your hotel or you can come and stay with me at my apartment."

She bit her lip unsure what to do. On one hand, she really wanted to stay with Lucas but on the other, being in the heart of Rome would be simpler.

"Where do you live? Is it close or far from the city?"

Silently he groaned as Tonio's warning came back. Thank God he not only heeded it and got Montana a room, but also upgraded it to a suite.

"At that question, I think you should stay at the hotel since I'll be working although I will take you to my apartment to show it to you."

The smile she gave him punched him in the stomach. She placed her palm on his cheek and looked deeply into his eyes.

"Thank you."

Her husky voice made him shiver and he kissed her once more.

"One more thing, I want you to meet my family before the engagement party, so do you think that you'll be up to having lunch with them tomorrow?"

"Oh, I —" She was flustered and anxious by the invitation. "O-okay."

"Great, I'll let my mother know."

He dropped her at the hotel and loved the look on her face when she was told she had been upgraded to a suite.

"I can't believe it," she said, excitedly twirling around the room. "First a private jet and now a suite, this is the best holiday ever and its only just started."

The heat and hunger in Lucas' eyes made her skin feel tingly all over as he walked towards her, slowly removing his jacket and then unbuttoning his shirt to reveal his chest.

"I believe you wanted to ogle an Italian hunk?"

"Oh yes." Her voice was breathless as she drooled, unable to take her eyes off him as he now stood proudly naked in front of her. "Oh my, my real own David come to life."

Her hands roamed all over him, feeling every curve and muscle. He was warm and hard *everywhere* and she couldn't stop touching him. He really was her own Italian god come to life.

Lucas was in agony at Montana's touch. He had never felt this aroused in his life as he let her touch brand him all over. He was desperate for her to undress so he could see what had only been in his dreams.

"Mon," he moaned. "I'm dying here."

He sucked in a breath when she took hold of his arousal unable to hold on for long as her mouth and hands were too skilful and he was also primed from missing her as she quickly brought him to his climax.

"Mon!"

"I wonder if all Italians are as hunky and virile as you?" She gave him a coquettish look. "Oh, the research I plan on doing."

His growl made her squeal as he lifted her up and proceeded to promptly divest her of her clothes so he could return the favour.

By the time he finished making her scream his name, he was looking deeply into her eyes as she caught her breath.

"I think its time we both came together again, don't you."

"Oh yes. Lucas, I've missed you so much."

Those were the last words spoken for a long time.

The next morning after a leisurely breakfast and more sex, she made sure to dress to impress, after all, she was meeting Lucas' family for the first time. She didn't remember being introduced to them in Spain and it felt rude even if most of her attention had been taken by either Lucas, or Marcos' sisters and their friend, Patrizia.

"Do I look all right?" she said, nervous. "I don't want to embarrass myself in front of your family."

He kissed her thoroughly to ease her worry.

"You look beautiful. My family isn't as snobby as Marco's. They'll love you. Besides, Giana will love you just for the fact you'll be distracting my mother from her and Petra even for a little while," he grinned.

She wasn't a hundred percent confident and the drive to his parents' house was filled with Lucas pointing out different sights that she may or may not know.

"I just love the Coliseum," she sighed.

"It is impressive, although I'm not sure about all the fighting and gladiators. Its romantic now but back then…"

"Good point. I'm not sure if I'd like to see people mauled alive by lions or pulled apart by horses," she said, horrified.

"Here we are, my parents' house."

"It's beautiful," she said in awe as they approached the mansion. "Now your parents are Franco and Alessia, and your sisters are Giana, Paola and Sofia." She was relieved she could remember all their names.

Lucas decided not to tell Montana she had already met Sofia on the beach in Spain. He silently hoped it might put Montana at ease, sort of breaking the ice if she recognised his sister.

As they entered the house, he prayed his family would be nice to Montana and they wouldn't look down their noses at her, since he now knew they had heard unkind things from his cousins.

Montana tightly held Lucas' hand and didn't relax until the introductions were made and she saw Sofia.

"I met you on the beach in Spain," she said, surprised. "What a small world. How is your friend's dog?"

Sofia beamed that Montana asked after the dog.

"Great. You have to meet my dog," Sofia said.

"Oh, are they here?" Montana said.

"Sì, he's somewhere probably digging up some of mamma's flowers."

"*Sofi*," Alessia chided, smiling. "He better not be, otherwise you'll be replacing them *all*."

"Sì, mamma," she smiled. "I'd better go check on Peppermint."

"Come and sit, Montana and tell us all about yourself," Alessia said.

They went into the lounge and Giana was there looking radiant holding a small baby.

"Oh, please, don't get up, you'll only sit back down again. I'm Montana and you must be Giana and Petra" she smiled.

Giana looked relieved Montana didn't expect her to rise.

"Sì. Welcome to Italy, I hear it's your first time here."

"Oh, I was briefly here for Marco's birthday but it was such a quick fly in and out visit that I didn't get to see anything so I'm hoping to do a lot more sightseeing this time," she said and then offered a wrapped package to her. "Toni and I bought Petra a present. We hope you like it."

"Grazie, you didn't have to do that," Giana said.

As she opened it, it was a beautiful woollen cashmere blanket and some baby toys.

"Oh, this is divine. Grazie Montana. I must remember to thank Toni too for your thoughtfulness," Giana said and then wrinkled her nose. "I think someone needs to be changed and have a nap."

As Giana left the room, the family interrogation began.

"So tell us about yourself Montana. All we know is that you are friends with Isabella and Antonia and come from New Zealand," Franco said.

Having Lucas sit beside her and holding her hand on the couch made her feel at ease.

"Gosh, I'm not sure what to say. I was born and grew up in New Zealand. I have five siblings…"

"Five siblings?" Paola said, surprised.

"Yes, Italians aren't the only ones who have big families," she laughed. "Okay, perhaps mine is bigger than most peoples."

"So brothers and sisters?" Franco said.

"I have three younger sisters and two younger brothers. I'm the eldest."

Lucas silently sat and let his family interrogate Montana so she could answer their questions and therefore his family could be reassured she was the real deal. He was ashamed to admit even he learned things about her that he didn't know, like the names of her siblings.

"My parents named us all after places in America since they loved it so much."

"I'd love to know what they are. Guiseppe and I constantly argued over baby names," Giana said, returning to the lounge without Petra. "My husband is off playing golf since he knew I was in good hands here at mamma's, at least that's what he says, but I know he just wants to get as many games in before I tell him to stop. I'm sure you'll get to meet him tonight at the party."

"We used to hate our names growing up but as we got older, we love them," she said. "Our names are like a party trick and normally we'd make people guess because they never can and its fun to watch them try to figure it out."

"So how long did Lucas take?" Paola said.

"Oh, I took it easy on him," she lied, not wanting his family to know he hadn't bothered to ask. "So I'm Montana, the eldest; next is Indiana or Indi for short; then there's Boston and Phoenix, my brothers; and bringing up the rear are Alexandria or Lexi and Savannah."

Seeing people's reactions to their names always made the Chan siblings laugh and Lucas' family were no different.

"Wow," Paola and Giana said together.

Lucas silently sat there realising he'd never asked Montana anything about her siblings apart from how many she had. In fact, he didn't know much about her personal life at all unless it was in relation to Toni and Izzy. Thankfully no one in his family knew Montana lied just to cover for him.

Sofia came back inside to join them and saw them all laughing and smiling.

"What did I miss?"

"First, how's my garden?" Alessia said, with a pointed look.

"Perfecto mamma. Peppermint would never dig up your flowers," she grinned. "Now what did I miss?"

"Montana was just telling us the names of her siblings," her mother said.

"Oh?" Sofia couldn't see what would be so interesting about that.

"While you ladies continue, Lucas and I have some things to discuss," Franco said.

Lucas looked at Montana who squeezed his hand and smiled.

"I'll be fine."

In front of everyone he made sure he kissed her with a possessiveness that shocked everyone, Montana included. Satisfied she looked dazed, he got up and went with his father.

"I-I'm…" She wasn't sure what to say, her cheeks burned with embarrassment and she was speechless as were all the other women in the room.

"I don't think I've ever seen Lucas act like that," Giana said.

"I don't think I've ever seen Lucas kiss a girlfriend like that," Paola said.

"I have," Sofia grinned as all eyes swung to her. "What? You should have seen them on the beach in Spain."

Montana felt herself go even redder, if it were possible.

"I'm so embarrassed. He's not, I mean, we don't normally...I'm sorry."

"Don't apologise," Alessia smiled. "We can take the hint. Seeing this side of him is interesting."

"What do you mean?" To her, Lucas was always like this.

"His possessiveness and protectiveness of you. I don't think I've ever seen him act that way before. Have you?" Alessia looked to her daughters who all shook their heads.

"Enough about Lucas and kissing," Sofia said, pulling an icky face. "Tell me what's so interesting about Montana's siblings?"

As they told her, Sofia's face was a picture and everyone was laughing.

Lunch was actually quite relaxing and it helped she could share stories from her childhood and even got to hold Petra until the baby started squawking and Montana panicked at what to do. Luckily Giana knew her daughter wanted food and took Petra to Montana's relief.

"So what do you think of my family? They seemed to like you *a lot*," he said, driving her back to the hotel so she could get ready for the engagement party.

"They're lovely and funny," she said. "Did I tell you that if Giana ever has a boy, she wants to call the him Rome."

"I'd love to see Giuseppe's face when she tells him that one. He'll probably have a heart attack." Lucas barked out a laugh.

"Why? What's wrong with Rome?"

"Nothing but Seppe's quite conservative so I'm imagining the baby will have a nice, normal, traditional name."

"Well, if she's smart she'll negotiate while she's in labour, then he won't be able to say no," she grinned.

"I'll remember that."

"What for?" she said, puzzled.

"Just in case you decide to do the same thing."

Her eyes widened at the implication and her heart accelerated in shock.

"Y-you think we'll have children…together?"

"Don't you?"

"I-I hadn't thought about it." Now she was flustered and feeling awfully hot, maybe she needed to wind the window down, but luckily they reached the hotel and she scrambled out of the car.

"Hey, what's with the panic?"

"I…you…us. It all seems so…" She wasn't sure what she was trying to say. They weren't even in a proper relationship.

He waited until they reached her room and to give her a chance to calm down before he spoke.

"Mon, from the moment I met you, I knew you were someone special," he said, cupping her face and looking deeply into her caramel eyes. "You feel the chemistry between us, too, right?"

"Y-yes, but we're not even a couple. We're bed buddies, remember? And now you've jumped about a thousand steps ahead while I'm still back at square one."

"Don't you want to get married and have children?"

To anyone else it was a foregone conclusion but how did she tell him she had already been married and buried a husband? She wasn't sure if she could go through all of that again. In fact, until Lucas brought it up right at this moment, she actually hadn't given it any thought at all. Now she could feel her panic rising quickly as she struggled to breath.

Her phone rang and she was grateful for the interruption.

"Hello?" she said. "Oh, okay, I'll let Lucas know. Thanks, Toni. I'll see you in a few hours."

She hung up and saw Lucas looking at her.

"Toni wanted to let us know that we should go a little bit earlier because Marco and Izzy would like to take some photos with just us."

Silently she thanked Toni for her timely interruption which not only neatly changed the subject, but also diffused the tension inside her.

He looked at his watch. The place where the engagement party was being held was at least a half hour to forty-five minute drive and he had to get home and dressed before coming back to pick Montana up.

"I'd better go and get ready then so I can come back and pick you up as well," he sighed, raking a hand through his hair.

"Is the place far away?"

"It's closer to my place than here."

"Would it be easier if I get ready at your place? That way you can show it to me at the same time?"

He knew she was just being practical but all he could imagine was having her in his bed and not wanting to leave.

"It would be easier but I don't think that it's the best idea."

"What? Why not?" she said, surprised.

He gave her one of his smouldering, *what do you think*, looks and she swallowed her breath.

"Oh," she said. "It's a shame that you're driving —"

"Fantastic idea. I don't know why I didn't think of this myself." He pulled out his phone and made a quick call. There was a lot of nodding and agreeing before he hung up.

"The limo will be downstairs waiting to take you and then it'll stop by my place on the way. This way I'll have you all to myself and no distractions," he grinned.

"I hope you can behave on the way there at least. On the way home, you can be as naughty as you like," she teased.

"Mon," he groaned. "Why do you say things like that? You're a tease and I'm now in agony."

"Well, since you're so efficient, I'm guessing you now have a little more time up your sleeve before you need to leave."

Just to ensure he got the message, she started to remove her dress.

"One day we are going to have a whole day, no a weekend, no a week, in bed with *no* interruptions," he growled, pouncing on her.

Chapter Fifteen

Montana was humming and smiling to herself as she got ready, wondering what it was about Lucas that made her feel sated and insatiable at the same time? It sounded like tonight was going to be as fabulous as the party in Spain with Lucas warning her this one would probably be bigger and more of a spectacle because knowing his family and more importantly, his Zia Rosa, it would be a very over-the-top celebration just like when her daughters got engaged and married. Then her thoughts drifted towards having to see Marco's sisters and their friend again.

No, she shook her head. She wasn't going to let those jealous women ruin her very good mood as she turned her thoughts back to Lucas. He had thrown her for a loop with the fact he could see them as a couple in the future, even with children. The thought honestly hadn't even entered her mind but now he brought it up, it also raised some terrifying thoughts she didn't think she'd even need to confront for years yet.

Deep down she knew if she really were truly ready to move forward with her life, it would be with Lucas. Just being together showed their unbelievable chemistry however, yet again, she was left wondering if that was all they had.

She still felt embarrassed as she answered all his family's questions knowing he hadn't even asked those same ones.

Deciding tonight wasn't the time for a deep and meaningful conversation or thoughts, she turned her mind to wondering what naughty mischief could be had in a limo. After all, if she and Lucas didn't end up together, at least she got incredible, spectacular sex.

Just the very thought made her excited and knowing she'd be at least kissing him, she left off her lipstick but ensured it was in her purse so she could put it on before they arrived, after all, there was no point having to do it twice and she didn't want Lucas to accidentally have lipstick on his collar.

Jangling with excited nerves, the limo reached Lucas' place and suddenly the door opened and she felt her breath whoosh right out of her body at the sight of him. Lucas in a tuxedo was genuinely the handsomest thing she had ever seen.

"You looking stunning." His eyes skimmed over her but the heat and desire she saw made her body tingle even more.

"So do you," she drooled. "Where's your tie? Do you need help?"

"I figured it would only get in the way and will put it on when we get there." His devilish smile ramped up the excitement she was feeling as he arched an eyebrow. "No lipstick?"

"No." She blushed. "Great minds must think alike. I thought it could end up dirtying your shirt so left it off for now."

"Hmm, I guess we do think alike. Come here," he said, hauling her into his lap and kissing her.

Just before they arrived, they were busily tidying themselves up and both held the same smouldering heated looks in their eyes every time they looked at each other, which made them both wish they were somewhere very private and with a bed.

It was going to be a long night and seeing their friends and family again was a welcome distraction.

As promised, Izzy and Marco took photos of them all together as a group and separate as friends or couples. Then Lucas and Tonio did their duty again with the Romero family photos giving Toni and Montana a chance to talk.

"How's it been with Tonio?"

"Oh, Mon." Toni gave a happy sigh. "It's been wonderful. These last couple of weeks have been like a wonderful dream I definitely don't want to wake from."

"So you two are definitely in it for the long haul?"

"Yes. I think the time we had apart made us realise we do want to be together, but it's the logistics now."

"It'll all work out," she said, confident. Toni and Tonio were definitely meant to be together.

"What about you and Lucas? I mean, you didn't want to stay with him." Toni looked anxious over the fact.

"We're fine, well, as fine as can be. We're bed buddies at the moment, although I did get to meet his family for lunch today and they were really lovely. By the way, Giana loved the present."

Toni didn't know whether to be shocked Montana was happy to just be sleeping with Lucas or excited that she met his family.

"I don't know what to say," she said. "You're not the kind of girl to just sleep around with a boy without a relationship."

"That sounds so teenager-ish," Montana giggled. "But I have to agree, I didn't think I was either but you know what, its spectacular and *hot*. Perhaps I should have done it years ago."

"I doubt it," Toni grinned. "That just wasn't you, and besides you had James."

"I know," she sighed.

Toni instantly felt guilty for bringing down Montana's happiness.

"Mon, I'm sorry, I shouldn't —"

"Don't be. I shouldn't get upset every time his name's mentioned especially when there's nothing I can do about it. It's just that times like now I feel stuck, you know — like its great I'm finally moving on with my life, but then it feels like I'm betraying James for forgetting about him and what we had together." Then she lowered her voice. "And if he hadn't died, I wouldn't be here with you guys and with someone so wonderful as Lucas. But I was happy with James and that's what makes everything so confusing."

Tears were welling in her eyes and Toni's guilt felt like a stone in her stomach as they hugged.

Out of the corner of Lucas' eye he could see Montana and Toni were both upset. Not caring whether he was required for the photo or not, he nudged Tonio and they both made their way over to their partners.

"Are you okay?" he said, sitting beside Montana and pulling her into his embrace.

"Yes, we're just having a little girlie chat and you know, we get a little emotional over all the excitement of being with you Romero boys," she said.

Although he knew Montana wasn't telling the entire truth, he let it go since she clearly didn't want him to know why she was upset.

"You'd better get back before they start looking for you," Toni said, kissing Tonio first.

"Somehow I don't think anyone would even notice. It's a zoo, if you haven't noticed," Tonio laughed.

They heard their names being shouted and the two women began laughing.

"Told you," Toni said.

Lucas gave Montana a very passionate kiss and she quickly wiped his mouth with her thumb.

"You don't want lipstick in the photos."

He winked and grabbed his cousin, pulling him away from Toni.

Just as Lucas warned, Izzy and Marco's Italian engagement party was a much more over-the-top affair than the one in Spain. There was also a lot more people in attendance and it was hard to find anyone in the crush.

Since it was also to be a sit-down dinner, Montana found herself on the same table as Toni and Izzy, Giana and Giuseppe — who she finally got to meet — and Marco's sister Allegra and her husband, Mattias.

It was a pleasant dinner and because she was seated next to Giuseppe, she got to know him a little better. He seemed like a lovely man and was constantly making sure Giana was comfortable.

"Your sister is very lucky," she said to Lucas as they danced. "Giuseppe is very doting."

"That's just appearances," he laughed. "I've heard stories that could curl your hair about those two and their fiery tempers."

"Really?" she said, surprised. "Neither strike me as the fiery type."

"I think having the baby may have calmed them down."

"I can't believe how many people are here tonight. It's quite a crush."

"Just means I get to hold you even closer."

His eyes flared with desire and she felt herself melting.

The night seemed to be going so well and with so many people to meet, she couldn't keep up with all the names and faces and how they were all connected. Since Lucas and Tonio knew most people, they socialised a lot, but Sofia and

Toni both kept Montana company with Sofia eager to introduce her to everyone as Lucas's girlfriend.

The only low point of the night was every time she looked for Lucas, she saw Patrizia Rossi standing next to him laughing and smiling.

"We tried to tell you they had an understanding. Now do you see how you don't fit in?" Pia said, siding up to her as Montana once again spotted Lucas and Patrizia together.

Although Montana didn't want to make a scene with Marco's sister, she wasn't willing to easily be defeated especially since Lucas assured her he had no interest in Patrizia and she believed him.

"Actually all I see is a desperate woman trying to cling to a man that doesn't want her."

"You will never be welcomed in this family," Pia hissed.

"Then it's a good thing you aren't a member of Lucas' immediate family."

The angry look on Pia's face at her reply made her slightly anxious, but she wasn't about to back down and apologise and before anything more could be said, Sofia came over.

"There you are Mon, there's someone I want you to meet."

"Lead the way," she said, grateful for Sofia's timely interruption.

"You cannot seriously be *friends* with *this* woman," Pia spat to her cousin.

"Why not? Unlike you, we all like her a whole lot more than Patrizia. You couldn't make Marco fall in love with her, and thank goodness, Lucas is also way too smart for that. Maybe Patrizia should actually try and find someone that likes her, which would be quite hard, since she's a bitch."

Montana stared gobsmacked at Sofia unable to believe her ears. Lucas' sister was not only defending her, but with such vehemence.

"How dare you talk to me like that?" Pia said. "Wait until I tell Zia Alessia."

"Mamma will agree entirely with me. Go and make someone else's life a misery, Pia."

Sofia pulled Montana away through the throng of people.

"I'm so sorry and thank you for defending me, but your family are going to be furious," she said, anxious.

"No, they won't. Pia is just like Zia Rosa — her mother — a snobby bitch who thinks they can manipulate and do whatever they want. And besides, what I said is true, we all like you and Patrizia is a bitch. Pia and Allegra tried to set her and Marco up years ago, although at the time Patrizia thought Marco was too immature and not wealthy enough. She was also just as horrid back then if all the snippets I overheard Marco telling Lucas were true."

Montana laughed. She understood eavesdropping younger siblings.

"Why they think Lucas would want her is beyond me. Patrizia could never fit into our family and Lucas would be miserable. What did Pia say to you anyway?"

Montana wasn't sure if she wanted to repeat what Pia said and cause more fuss.

"She was just being spiteful. Thanks again for sticking up for me." Impulsively she hugged Sofia and was happy she had at least one person besides Lucas in her corner, more if Lucas' family truly did like her as Sofia suggested. "Now who did you want me to meet?"

Finally Montana and Lucas were in the limo away from the noise and able to use the privacy to their advantage.

"Did you enjoy yourself tonight?" he said, nuzzling her neck and she felt her breath beginning to quicken as her heart sped up.

"It was great. I saw Patrizia was by your side a lot of the time."

She hadn't wanted to mention it and seem jealous, but she also needed to clear the air and ensure it was all innocent.

"She kept following me and inserting herself into every conversation. It was annoying and rude," he said, looking deeply into her eyes so she would know he wasn't interested in Patrizia in any way.

"I know," she sighed. "I think I just wanted to make sure. Did I tell you that Sofia came to my rescue when Pia was being spiteful?"

"No, but I heard that Zia Rosa was having an argument with mamma only no one knew what about."

"Oh no," she said, concerned. "I think that's because of me. You see, Pia was being mean and Sofia stuck up for me and in the process said some things that your cousin took offence at. Pia did say that she was going to tell your mother about Sofia's rudeness to her."

Lucas blew out a breath realising what happened.

"I'm guessing Pia told Zia Rosa instead because in her eyes, the girls are all angels and are never at fault."

"Maybe I should call your mother and tell her that it wasn't Sofia's fault, that she was just defending me."

Seeing how upset Montana was, and knowing that his mother knew what his aunt was like and would have asked Sofia for her version of the incident, he decided the best course of action for them both was distraction.

"I believe you said that I'm allowed to be very naughty in the limo on the way home." He gave her a devilish grin and kissed her so all thoughts other than passion flew out of her head.

Never had a car ride been so erotic and by the time they reached her hotel they were both mussed and Montana barely knew her name.

They rushed to her room, laughing and touching and kissing the whole way until they finally made it to the bed.

Lucas was lying in bed unable to believe just how perfect Montana was for him. She was independent and not clingy or needy like some of his previous girlfriends. She also wasn't trying to constantly ingratiate herself with his family or trying to drop hints and talk about their future together. In fact, he was the one to bring it up to her shock. He also couldn't overlook the fact that the sex was scorching hot every time.

This is what made her the perfect woman for him, yet somewhere deep down in his stomach there was a strange sensation he'd never felt before.

Holding her closely to him, he kissed the top of her head and wondered if he could get Montana to stay until next weekend since they were going to have a baby celebration for Petra.

Somehow, during the night, Montana found herself agreeing to stay for another week for Giana's baby celebration, although she easily let Lucas seduce her into it.

"Are you sure she's up for it?" she said, knowing it was going to be a big family affair.

Lucas was surprised by the concern in Montana's voice.

"I don't think its usually this close to the birth but because most of the family are already here because of Marco's engagement, they thought it would be easier to get it over with instead of everyone having to come back."

"Don't they have jobs to get to?"

"It's a family business so most of them were going to be hanging around this week to do family business stuff anyway," he chuckled. "Now enough about that, let's get back to us."

After another long leisurely satisfying bout of sex, they both fell asleep until Montana's restlessness woke Lucas.

"Pasta," she murmured, smiling in her sleep.

Lucas couldn't help but smile and held her tighter to him.

"Hmm, love you…"

His smile widened even more.

"James."

His body froze at what she'd said in her sleep. Who the hell was James and why was she saying his name and that she loved him in her sleep?

Montana woke up and felt all out of sorts like she hadn't had a wink of sleep all night. She dreamt of James much like that time on San Miguel and wondered why. Then she realised she was alone in the bed. Where was Lucas?

On the table beside her was a note saying he had to leave and go away for work for a few days, but he'd see her when he got back.

She frowned. He hadn't mentioned a business trip. Maybe it was just something he forgot about. Disappointed he hadn't even woken her to say goodbye, she lay there thinking about James and knew it was now time to move on. She'd never forget him but with Lucas, she felt like she had her whole life ahead of her.

Chapter Sixteen

Montana's curiosity finally got the better of her after seeing an elderly man sitting outside in the hotel's garden at the same time for the past few days. Deciding today she was going to meet him, she still felt guilty about intruding and yet, sensed perhaps he might also be lonely and like a friend.

"Ciao," she said, as she approached so not to startle the man who looked in deep thought.

Silently she hoped she was doing the right thing intruding on this man's quiet time.

The man looked up at her and smiled but said nothing.

"I hope you don't mind me intruding on your peace and quiet, but it's such a lovely day and I thought I'd come and enjoy this lovely garden area," she said.

Again, the man said nothing but waved her to sit down and share the seat beside him although there were plenty of other empty and unused bench seats dotted around the garden area.

"I'm Montana."

The thought she was talking to someone who didn't understand a word she was saying made her flush a little with embarrassment.

"Gianni."

The man's voice was so quiet Montana thought she hadn't heard him properly because the wind carried his voice away, before noting there was no wind at all.

The feeling of relief the man did indeed understand English made her relax and smile brightly.

"It's lovely to meet you, Gianni. Are you just visiting Rome like me?"

Gianni gave a little chuckle to himself. After overhearing some of the things his grandchildren were saying about Lucas' new girlfriend, he decided to do a little snooping of his own. He hadn't met her at the engagement party but then, there were so many people he didn't think he saw half of those in attendance.

Normally he wouldn't bother, but everyone seemed to be in some sort of rivalry and he, himself wanted to make sure this woman was good enough for his grandson. Secretly he didn't doubt she was, after all, Tonio and Marco's partners were her friends and Lucas was no dummy when it came to women.

He also knew some of what he overheard was just spiteful jealousy from Pia, Allegra and Patrizia Rossi. Still it wouldn't hurt to find out more about this Montana everyone was talking about and it gave him a chance to feel useful.

Gianni's son and daughter-in-law, Franco and Alessia seemed to like Montana and clearly Lucas did too, but that didn't mean the woman wasn't just a good actress and so he instigated the subterfuge of him being a guest at the hotel in hopes of meeting her and she didn't disappoint.

"Yes and no. I used work here and have lunch out here every day with my wife." There was sadness in Gianni's eyes and a wistfulness in his voice.

"Oh, I'm so sorry. Has your wife passed away?" she said, hoping Gianni didn't think she was prying.

"Five years ago and I still miss her every day. That's why I come here, to remember her." He felt guilty for partly lying to Montana about why he was at the hotel after seeing her compassion for him, however, he did like to come to the gardens and reminisce about his Allegra and their wonderful life together.

Montana's heart went out to Gianni. It must be even harder to lose someone special when you were older. She understood since she lost James but knew she was still young enough to remarry, have a family and build a new life with someone else which gave her hope and helped ease the sadness she sometimes felt.

"Were you married long?"

"Sixty wonderful years."

"Wow, that's amazing," she said. "What about your children or grandchildren? Do you see them much?" She felt guilty asking such a personal question. "I hope you don't think that I'm being nosy."

"I see them often but…" Gianni's quiet voice trailed off.

"I completely understand. It's not the same as having your wife by your side every day."

The older man looked over at the young lady with almost glistening eyes as he nodded at Montana's insight.

"I'm so sorry. I didn't mean to upset you," she said.

"Oh no, you haven't," he said, wiping the little moisture from his eyes with a hanky. "I'm a little surprised by your insight but you see today, well, today was our anniversary and I was feeling a little alone, but then you came and made me feel like my Allegra is here with me."

"Oh." She was unsure what to say. On one hand it was a lovely compliment and she was very glad she decided to come and talk to Gianni today and on the other, she felt sad for him as well. She looked at her watch. "Oh no, I'm supposed to be meeting my friends shortly. I'm so sorry but I have to go. Will you be all right here by yourself?"

Gianni smiled, pleased by Montana's kindness.

"Of course. Thank you for caring."

"Will you be here tomorrow? I'd love to talk to you some more," she said, happy she managed to hopefully cheer Gianni up a little.

"Yes, and I shall look forward to it." Gianni beamed. "Thank you for making my day, Montana. Perhaps you'll tell me all about yourself tomorrow."

"It's a deal. I'll see you tomorrow."

Gianni watched Montana leave and speak to one of the hotel employees. He knew she was talking about him because of the way she looked and pointed discreetly in his direction. Wondering what she was doing, he was surprised to find himself being offered a lovely piece of cake, compliments of the hotel.

Since the hotel employee was one of his nephew's children, he said, "Dante, is the hotel really giving me a complimentary piece of cake or did the lady you just talked to earlier pay for it?"

"Guess there's no fooling you, Zio Gianni," Dante grinned. "She said you needed a bit of cheering up and was there a piece of cake or some sort of sweet treat we could give you. When I told her that no, we just don't give out such things, so she said she'd go inside and order you something, but we had to pretend it was from the hotel."

"I thought so," he smiled.

"How do you know her?" Dante said, curious.

"Actually I've just met her."

"And she's buying you cake?" Dante looked surprised.

Gianni just continued smiling trying to decide whether Montana was a very good actress who perhaps knew who he really was or was just a kind, caring person — perfect for his grandson.

Montana and Gianni spent the next few days of her stay having afternoon tea together outside in the garden. She told the older man about growing up in New Zealand with five siblings all named after various different places in America.

She also told Gianni about James and how hard it was to lose him at such a young age, more so because it had been so sudden.

Gianni's heart went out to Montana at that tragic circumstance. At least he had most of his life together with Allegra and it made him even more thankful.

"And that's what brought me here now," she said, finishing her life story.

"Well, I'm glad that you're moving on with your life and am very glad to have met you. I'll be sad to see you go," Gianni said, with sincerity. He enjoyed talking to the young woman every day. No matter what the rest of his family thought, he knew she was right for his family and especially Lucas. She wasn't this evil, gold-digging woman his granddaughters liked to think. If anyone was, it would be Patrizia Rossi, their friend.

"I know, me too," she said, glum. "Although I'm sad to be leaving, I don't quite know what the future holds."

"What do you mean?"

She shouldn't have said anything, but it seemed she just needed to let it out to someone who hopefully wouldn't think she was crazy.

"You see, my best friend Izzy is engaged to Marco and Marco's sisters aren't the most pleasant women I've met."

"Is your friend not accepted by these sisters?"

"Oh no, Izzy's fine. It's just that, you see, I like Marco's cousin, Lucas *a lot* but they have their sights on Lucas being with their best friend, Patrizia and so they all like to make snide remarks when I see them, which thankfully is not often."

"It's jealousy," he said.

"I totally agree so I laugh it off, even ignore it when I can, but I guess what's really on my mind is this whole thing with Lucas. We're not quite a couple, as such and yet, I do want to be with him but…"

"Does this have anything to do with your James?"

Unable to help herself, she burst into tears.

"I'm sorry."

"No, I'm sorry, I didn't mean to make you cry."

"You haven't. It's just that I dreamt about James the other night. It was similar to one I had when I first met Lucas and now I feel ready to move on, but Lucas suddenly went away for work and I've hardly heard from him in the past few days," she said, morose.

"Now I understand. Does Lucas know about James?"

"No."

"He doesn't know?" Gianni looked stunned by the news.

"I don't know how to tell him. You see, we met on holiday and it wasn't anything more than a fling, as such. Then we met up again and I don't know where this thing between us is going so I'm not sure…I mean, how do you tell someone something like that?"

"I understand," he said, patting her hand.

"The other hard thing is that he doesn't seem to ask me any questions about my life. I know it sounds like I'm being self-centred but I'm not, I promise. It's just that I met his family, who were lovely, and they seemed more interested in me than him. I know they're just making sure I'm good enough for him, but the fact he hasn't asked any of these questions, well, it just makes me sad when I think about it, so I try not to."

"I see. So you think that Lucas is only using you as a...*bed buddy*?" he said, hesitant, wondering why his grandson wasn't asking all those personal questions, when Montana seemed quite an open person.

"That's just it, why it's so confusing," she said, shaking her head. "He was the one who brought up the fact he could see us having kids."

Gianni could still sense the shock of Lucas' comment on Montana's face.

"What did you say to that?"

"I was speechless. I haven't had any kind of thoughts about that stuff at all since James died. That's why I'm so confused. He doesn't seem to want to get to know me personally but is ready to imagine us with children?"

"I understand where you're coming from," he nodded. "I don't mean to be nosy but is your friend, Izzy, Marco Romero's fiancée?"

"Yes, how did you know?" she said, surprised and feeling uncomfortable as her face felt hot. Had she just spilt her secrets to someone she shouldn't have?

"Then I'm guessing the Lucas you are talking about is Lucas Romero?"

"Yes. Do you know them?" Now she was feeling very wary but then shooed the thought away since Gianni seemed like a nice grandfatherly man, not some kind of top secret spy.

"I'm more interested in knowing how you met them," he said, ignoring her question.

"My best friends and I met the boys on holiday in San Miguel."

"I see."

"You do?" Now she was one who was confused.

"So Marco's other cousin, Antonio is dating your other friend?"

"Yes, Toni. They're such a cute couple, Tonio and Toni," she sighed.

"If you don't mind my nosiness, do you like Lucas because you like him or because your friends are with his cousins?"

"His being cousins with my best friends' partners is a bonus but Lucas is...I'm not sure how to describe him. He's...a good friend," she lamely said. "Like I said, I'm totally confused about this whole thing...and James. How am I supposed to break it to him since we're not really dating, *oh and by the way, I've been married and am now a widow*. He'll have a heart attack."

While Gianni only nodded, it seemed to Montana the older man appeared to understand something that perhaps she didn't.

"You mentioned meeting Lucas' family, do you know what they think of you?"

"To be honest, they've been really nice...but who knows? Maybe they don't think I'm the right type of woman for their son and brother and are praying hard nothing comes of this, although Lucas' younger sister, Sofia definitely likes me. She even stood up for me at Marco's engagement when one of her cousins was being unkind," she said, but then looked thoughtful. "But like I said earlier, the Romero family are a very close-knit family so... What happens if they don't like the fact that I've already been married and widowed?"

Heaving a loud sigh she thought of Lucas. She really did need to tell him about James, but he seemed so cold on the phone the one time he rang and she wasn't sure if it was work stress or something else. Besides, she wasn't about to tell him something so personal unless it was face to face.

Gianni rubbed his chest feeling out of sorts.

"Are you alright?" she said.

"I don't feel very well all of a sudden."

Montana looked at Gianni, noting that he did look very pale.

"What is it? Is it your heart?" She could feel the panic rapidly rising inside her.

"Just give me a minute and I'll be fine. Sometimes I just don't feel right, that's all. Maybe it's too much sun."

It wasn't an unusually hot day, she thought, trying hard to remain calm sitting there with him. As time slowly past, she couldn't help but note that he didn't seem to be getting any better.

"I'm getting an ambulance."

"Don't be silly, I'll be fine."

"No, it could be a heart attack and I'll feel better if you get to a hospital and they say I'm overreacting."

She found a hotel employee and asked them to call an ambulance. Upon hearing someone in their hotel was having a medical emergency they sprang into action and also got the hotel doctor to come.

Before Montana knew what was happening, the ambulance arrived and the doctor was certain Gianni was indeed having either a heart attack or at least the warning symptoms of one, but they'd know more once he was at the hospital.

Since Montana didn't know Gianni, she couldn't go with him to the hospital but felt better knowing the hotel would contact anyone in his family on his behalf.

Walking to her room in a daze and upset, she entered only to realise she was trembling in shock.

What if she had listened to Gianni and not called for help? Would he be all right? Did they get him the medical help he needed in time or was it just a warning? She prayed hard it was just a warning. The trauma of what happened to James came flooding back and she broke down in tears.

Chapter Seventeen

Lucas was upset by the news his grandfather was in the hospital after having an extremely mild heart attack, which luckily was not only caught early but meant his nonno would now have continual monitoring.

His first thoughts of anxiousness and concern gave way to needing Montana to be here with him.

Deciding this was more important than his aggravation over her talking in her sleep and saying she loved another man, he had his driver take him to the hotel to see her all the while refusing to admit this was the justification he needed to break his stubbornness about not talking to her earlier.

Knocking on her door, she opened it surprised to see him.

"Lucas! What are you doing here? I thought you were away until Friday?"

"I thought that you might like to spend the remainder of your time at my place?" he said, ignoring her questions.

Before she could answer, he kissed her with so much ferocity she almost stumbled from the force and then held her closely to him.

"I-I…we never really discussed —"

He silenced her with another bruising kiss.

"Pack up all your stuff, we'll take it with us."

"Okay," she said, dazed. "How have you been? How was your trip?"

He didn't want to talk about such mundane things when his grandfather was ill before realising Montana didn't know, that he actually hadn't told her. Deciding it was nice to have a distraction, he watched her pack quickly and efficiently and he told her of his trip.

What he hadn't told her was there had been no work trip until he decided to take one. After hearing Montana say another man's name — one that wasn't her brothers' — in her sleep, he needed time away to get his thoughts in order and to calm his anger down before he confronted her.

Now with his grandfather in hospital, it still wasn't the right time and if he wasn't being stupid, he would have left her to stay in the hotel but for some perverse reason, he wanted her in his bed.

A niggle of doubt made him wonder if she was playing him.

"I can't wait to see your place. I bet its lovely," she said.

"I'm sure you'll love it."

The car came to a stop and because she hadn't been looking out the window, she assumed they reached their destination until she stepped out and realised that this wasn't Lucas' place.

"Where are we?"

"Hospital. My nonno's had a very mild heart attack, more of a warning doctors apparently said, and I thought we'd stop in and see him first."

"H-hospital?" she whispered, her voice trembling.

She walked up to the entrance and stopped, standing there just looking at the automatic doors as if they were the mouth to a nightmare. People were casually entering and exiting with no idea about what could happen inside, they didn't have any problems with the building but her feet refused to budge and she sat on the nearest seat.

"I can't do it."

Fear and memories of the last time she was at a hospital with James paralysed her. She couldn't do it, her heart was pounding and zooming, but this wasn't like when she was making love to Lucas, this was far worse and she started to hyperventilate and tremble.

Lucas, who entered and assumed she was following, came out to find her looking ashen and panicky and sat next to her.

"Are you okay?"

"I-I can't go inside, I'm sorry," she whispered, trying hard to speak and keep breathing.

"Why not? It's just a hospital," he said, not understanding her fear.

"I'm sorry, I just can't."

"My grandfather's in there and needs his family around him. I'll be with you. Come." He stood and offered her his hand but she shook her head. "I don't have time for this, my family need me," he said, irritable and strode towards the doors stopping to take one last look back to see if she changed her mind, but she was still sitting there staring at the ground and he continued inside.

Raking a hand through his hair he couldn't understand what the problem was. Montana was all about family or so she said and yet the one time he really needed her, she bailed on him. He was angry at her selfishness and didn't have time to worry about what her problem was.

Right now, he needed to be strong for his family and grandfather. Tonio and Toni both came, as did Marco and Isabella making Montana's absence even more glaringly obvious, but the women didn't say anything and his cousins took him to one side to ask him where she was.

"Hey, how's nonno?" Lucas said, looking as solemn and worried as everyone else it the waiting room.

"Okay, he's resting for now. Now we just have to wait to see what if any, long term effects there might be," Marco said.

"Where's Montana?" Tonio said.

It was an innocent question but it made him angry all the same. Lucas really didn't want to go into it but Izzy overheard and also wanted to know.

"She's downstairs, I think." He hardly got the words out before Izzy was tapping Toni on the shoulder to follow her. Lucas just assumed they were going to give her a much needed dressing down and was quite happy for them to make her see sense, if that was possible.

They found her outside sitting on a bench. She hadn't moved and there were tears on her cheeks she quickly brushed away when she saw her friends coming.

"You need to tell him," Izzy said, insistent as Toni agreed.

"No, I can't, not now," she said, shaking her head. "He needs to concentrate on his grandfather. I can't just load him up with my phobia of hospitals because I have a dead husband. What am I supposed to say? By the way Lucas, I have a dead husband and only now do I realised that I'm too afraid to go into a hospital?" Her self-deprecating manner just showed them how miserable she was. "He'll think I'm an idiot. Even *I* didn't even know until tonight that I couldn't go in, that I'd have a panic attack."

"He'll understand," Toni said.

Montana almost laughed hysterically.

"No, he won't and I don't expect him too. He needs to focus on his grandfather and family. You guys go and be the great Romero partners you are, supporting them through this. I'll just roll with the punches."

The sadness in her eyes was almost too much for her friends to bear. Montana didn't deserve this but what she said was true, they needed to be with their men. Reluctantly, they left her sitting there alone and lost.

When Lucas saw the two women return with worry on their faces, any hope he had was lost when he saw Montana wasn't with them. An inner rage simmered and he squashed it down roughly, choosing to ignore the feeling of abandonment when his cousins had their partners' love and support.

Montana stayed outside until it was too cold to remain. She hadn't wanted to leave, but the chill was biting through her thin dress and she had no choice but to go to Lucas' house.

Luckily his driver was happy to take her and feeling tired and drained, and knowing Lucas would be angry, she didn't take in any of her surroundings and just found a spare bed, not wanting to be rejected by him.

Lucas came home, alone and when he got to his room, he was prepared for an argument but Montana wasn't there. He looked for her through the rooms and finally found her asleep in one of the guest beds. She looked like an angel and he couldn't fail to see the dried tears on her cheeks and that made his heart tug, but he refused to feel sympathy for her. Leaving the room quietly, he went back to his room to sleep, his thoughts all on Montana.

The next morning, she found him already at the table having breakfast as she walked in and hesitantly sat down.

"How's your grandfather?" she said, her voice barely a whisper.

"Don't tell me you're trying to pretend that you care, cara," he mocked. "If you did, you would have come to see for yourself."

"I told you, I *don't do* hospitals," she said, defensive and stubborn. "Maybe I should just go back home," she sighed. "You've obviously got a lot on your plate and us arguing isn't helping."

He felt a sudden surge of panic swirl around him at her words, unsure why since what she said was true. Heck even he thought it himself but now it was out there, he didn't want her to go.

Much to his chagrin, he needed her last night. Needed her naked and sobbing his name when he brought her to climax, but she chose to sleep elsewhere.

"So you're not going to bother staying until Sunday?"

Lucas' indifferent tone made her heart squeeze.

"Didn't you just hear what I said? All we'll do is spend the next few days arguing, like we are now. Maybe I should go back to the hotel if it's that important to you," she said, not really wanting to, but she didn't want to be beaten over the head with the fact she wasn't going into the hospital.

"I was also counting on you for a business dinner I have, not just the Romero family celebrations."

"That was before and since I'm not really family, it won't matter if I'm not there anyway."

"Yes, but it's for family *and friends* so you count," he said, before adding his last little guilt-trip. "I thought you wanted to spend as much time as you can with Izzy and Toni?" He arched an eyebrow at her and she knew she was beaten. Lucas was just trying to keep his cousins happy and if she left, Izzy and Toni would be asking questions of him.

Now that Toni and Tonio had made up, Toni decided she was going to move to Italy, leaving Montana the only one left in England.

"I'm really sorry Mon, but I have to give this a proper go.

Tonio said that if it really doesn't work out then he'll move to London for me."

Toni had been apologetic but so deliriously happy that Montana wanted to cry at the feeling of being abandoned but she couldn't deny her best friend a chance at happiness while pretending she wasn't the slightest bit envious of Izzy or Toni's good fortunes.

"I don't have to go to the hospital and you're not going to pressure me about it?" she said, wary.

"Fine."

He agreed too readily for her liking. Had she just walked into some kind of trap?

"One more thing," he said, so casually like it was an afterthought but she knew better. She looked at him and waited. "No more sleeping in any other bed but mine. Have we got that clear?"

"As crystal," she mumbled.

"Good, now we have a dinner tonight. I have a credit card for you so you'll need to make sure that you have something appropriate to wear."

He tossed a credit card at her and suddenly Montana felt like she couldn't breathe, she had just agreed to become his mistress without even realising it.

Lucas left for the hospital and then work while she went back to the room and wept. That's all she seemed to be doing these days is sleep and cry. She must be just out of sorts from everything that happened.

Although she was glad Lucas' grandfather was doing better, her thoughts came around to Gianni — the man from the hotel — and she wondered how she could get a bunch of flowers to him since she wasn't family nor was she planning on visiting the hospital. Deciding the first step was to call the hospital to see if he was even still there before getting his room number.

She ended up getting the florist to deliver a small bouquet with a sunflower in the centre to hopefully bring a smile to his face.

By late morning she was bored with shopping — something she didn't like doing at the best of times but not feeling a hundred percent just made it worse. Nothing seemed to fit properly or suit her and as time passed she ended up buying the first little black dress that looked even halfway decent on her. It showed off her cleavage in a classy yet understated way thanks to the draping, and clung to her curves. She couldn't believe how her breasts looked in the dress. While she wasn't one for ample cleavage, this dress really enhanced what she had to make her look sexier. She decided to buy it as Italian designers really know how to dress the female form.

Going back to Lucas', she asked for a salad for lunch from his housekeeper and then went for a sleep. By the time she woke, he had left a message he'd be back by seven for dinner. As she got ready, she saw how pale she was and covered it up with make-up.

Slipping into her dress, she found having to go braless was making her nipples quite sensitive as the dress rubbed them every time she moved making her fidget, something she hadn't noticed in the shop as she did only just try it on, thought it looked the part and then bought it.

She was doing her hair when Lucas entered the room and tossed his tie onto a nearby chair before starting to unbutton his shirt. She looked at him with unashamed hunger as if she was a starving person looking at a sumptuous feast and it made her subconsciously lick her lips.

"Don't look at me like that, tesoro or we'll never make it to dinner," he drawled, his eyes flickering with desire.

She could only blush at being so obviously caught out ogling him. He came up behind her and she could feel the heat from his half naked body.

"You know I'm only going to be thinking of getting you home and out of that incredible dress," he said, nibbling on her ear sending shivers all over her body before leaving her for a quick shower. Her legs had gone all wobbly at his words and she was thankful he didn't see just how much he affected her.

Lucas sat through dinner trying hard to concentrate on the table conversation, but it was extremely difficult as all he could think all night was that Montana's dress was indecent. Yes, she was covered up compared to Michael Cannelli's date, Petra Valente who was almost falling out of her dress, but Lucas could see the outline swell of Montana's lusciously ripe-looking breasts. Her puckered nipples showed through the material and he knew Michael also noticed because his eyes much like his own were constantly being drawn to her chest. The bodice could have been curtains and if you pulled the material to one side, then you'd have your own personal peep show. What had Montana been thinking when she bought that dress — to have the men at the table aroused all evening?

Finally he had her where he wanted her, in his bedroom, alone.

"That dress is completely indecent, cara mia." His husky voice and wolfish grin left her in no doubt that he wanted her.

"B-but I'm totally respectable and covered up."

How he could be so turned on by her dress when Petra's dress had bombshell written all over it?

"Every man in the room wanted to know just how luscious your breasts were under that dress." He scowled at the thought of all the stares she received as she walked through the restaurant.

She gasped at his blatantly sexual remark, her face feeling hot and her breasts — traitorous that they were — strained for his touch.

"Stop being so crude. Of course they didn't," she said, as he came closer.

"Shall I tell you then what every man including myself, saw?"

His eyes darkened with desire and she couldn't look away, trapped by wanting to know and yet, she felt so naive and innocent. She stood there saying nothing and he continued on tracing his finger down her décolletage before cupping an unfettered breast.

"The soft swelling of your chest even though hidden by the well draped material teased us every time you moved, knowing you had no bra on and yet, they are so pert and full," he said, rubbing his thumb over her nipple making moisture pool between the tops of her thighs as she tried hard not to feel affected by his touch.

"The tease of your skin here."

He trailed a finger between the shallow valley of her breasts and she shivered as he reached behind her and unzipped her dress just enough to loosen the bodice before sliding down the straps to let the front fall and revealing the objects of desire.

"Just as they hoped that you would uncover yourself to show them what it was they coveted. Perfect."

He devoured her unfettered breasts with his eyes, cupping them once more before bending his head to capture his reward.

Montana almost came on the spot at his seduction and the feel of his hot mouth on her breast. He nipped and suckled first one breast and then the other and she wanted to feel him, have him naked and in her. Her body was demanding his touch...demanding more.

He turned her around and kissed her neck and shoulders as he finished unzipping her dress and letting it fall to the floor. Seeing that she was only wearing a skimpy pair of lacy black panties, his erection was now hard as granite so she leant back onto him, arching against him, signalling her need for him.

He quickly stripped his clothes and she couldn't help but admire such a god-like physique. Running her hands everywhere over his torso before kneeling before him to worship him, he didn't want that tonight, tonight he just needed to be in her warmth, having her beg him.

Laying her back on the bed, he once again teased her breasts and then placed his head between her thighs. The first flick of his tongue against her very sensitive nub made her undone and she grabbed his head tightly, begging.

"*Lucas, please...*"

"What do you want, tesoro? *Tell me*," he rasped against her sex, as he tasted even more of her.

"Oh God. You! I just want you!"

The desperation in her voice matched his own inner turmoil as he thrust into her and she screamed his name to the world.

Her inner muscles clenched all around him sucking him into the vortex of her climax and causing him to cry out her name in return.

Montana lay next to Lucas with all her nerve endings still prickling. That was one of the most intense moments she ever had and yet, it didn't feel like enough. She was craving more but her eyelids were heavy and she fell asleep not waking until the morning.

Lucas was amazed Montana slept so deeply and noted that since they made up she was looking more gaunt, ashen and tired. Maybe he should get a doctor to check her out, but then decided against it since she was only here until Sunday.

Chapter Eighteen

Montana caught up with Izzy and Toni for lunch and as they happily chatted about Petra's baby celebration, it also sounded like grandfather Romero would be discharged from the hospital in the next day or two. Unfortunately, he wouldn't be in attendance at the party even if he was discharged in time.

They were discussing dresses with both Izzy and Toni saying they were having designer dresses made specifically for them. Montana said nothing, she didn't seem to have the same kind of loving relationship like her best friends. In fact apart from sex with Lucas at night, they didn't share much else. Deep down she knew she loved him, but he didn't love her so she kept it to herself not wanting to spoil their lunch.

On Saturday she wasn't feeling well but just put it down to nerves and after a while it seemed to go away. Still she decided to make sure she took the day easy as Lucas went into work for a few hours so she just rested.

"I have a present for you," he said, coming into the bedroom with a dress bag.

"Oh?" She tried not to get excited over it.

"I had this made for you." He unzipped the bag and revealed a beautiful fuchsia one-shoulder dress made of silk.

"It's beautiful," she said, unable to take her eyes off it as she became teary at his thoughtfulness.

"Are you crying?" he said, surprised.

"N-no. I-I just got something in my eye." She quickly wiped her eyes as he grinned.

Slipping it on, it felt like a dream and she put her hair up making her feel glamorous. She couldn't wear underwear under it as it would show and wondered if Lucas had done it on purpose before she smiled to herself that it didn't matter, as it would drive him crazy all night.

"You look gorgeous," he said, his eyes heated in desire.

She gave him a kiss thank you and as he ran his hands down her dress he was pretty sure Montana wore nothing under it making him instantly hard at the thought. Damn, now he needed to think of icebergs, freezing cold icebergs. What was he thinking getting her such a sexy dress? Next time he'd get her a sack and even that made him smile to himself knowing even if she were wearing a sack, he still wouldn't be able to keep his hands off her.

They left for the party and Montana started hyperventilating the moment she saw they pulled up to the hospital.

"Wh-what are we doing here?" she croaked, her chest constricting tightly making it hard for her to breath.

"I need to see my grandfather. Come up with me?" he said, knowing he had done it on purpose to get her to come.

"N-no. I-I'll wait here."

A scowl crossed his face.

"I thought we were over this nonsense," he said, irritated.

"If you want to go in and say goodnight, go ahead but I'm *not* going in."

"Fine," he snapped, hopping out of the limo as she burst into tears feeling like a fool because she couldn't do something which would not only make Lucas happy, but meant a lot to him.

When he returned, the limo was filled with stony silence and tension. Upon their arrival at the party, he helped her out of the car but his demeanour was now stiff and tense. A wall had gone up around him and she couldn't help but wish she hadn't come. He stayed by her side out of politeness but at the first chance to leave, he took it and didn't return, making her feel like unwanted leftovers.

"Oh dear, trouble in paradise?" Patrizia smirked. "I heard the you two weren't getting along. Every time *I've* been to the hospital to visit, I and everyone noted *you* haven't visited once. The family are most upset and hoping since you clearly don't have the same family values as the rest of us, Lucas will dump you like a hot potato. Even his grandfather wasn't pleased at all by your lack of support, but don't worry, I've been consoling Lucas."

Ignoring the jealous woman, and needing to grab some

breathing space she went out onto the patio and tried to hold back the tears. She just managed to calm herself when someone tapped her on the shoulder.

"Montana? Is that you?" a male voice said.

Turning, she was looking into a face she instantly recognised and felt comfortable with.

"Stephen! What are you doing here?" she said, stunned to see James' brother. She hadn't realised he was in Europe.

"To tell you the truth, I have no idea." He shook his head baffled. "My boss at work got invited and asked me if I wanted to come in his place since he couldn't make it and had already accepted. It sounded exciting at the time, but now I kind of feel out of place since I hadn't realised this was also a baby celebration, the invite made it sound like it was a business thing. How are you doing?" he said, concerned.

"Okay." She pasted a strained smile on her face. "I can't believe you're here, in Italy. How long have you been in Europe?"

"Not long, just a few months. I managed to do a sneaky intercompany transfer so I didn't have to pay to come over and they also found me a great place to live in Ireland," he chuckled.

"Ireland?"

"Yes, our company global headquarters is in Ireland. Better tax breaks," he grinned. "It's really good to see you again, Mon. How come you're here?" He raised an eyebrow in curiosity.

"An extremely long story," she said, morose.

"Want to talk about it?"

Everyone in the Dobson family knew how devastated Montana was when James died. It was nice to see she seemed to be moving on with life again. He couldn't even imagine how hard it it had been for her.

"I don't know," she sighed. "It's pretty complicated."

"Since when do you girls do anything but?" he teased, making her smile. "Which one is he? Do I need to talk to him?" He postured, making her giggle.

"No, this is my mess, I need to tell him the truth only there never seems to be a good time," she said, sober.

"Ah…James." He nodded his understanding.

"Yes. I don't think he'll take it well."

"Well, I'm in town until Tuesday if you need me. Give me a call, okay?" he said, offering his business card.

Montana took it and saw Stephen's company title was very impressive, he truly had moved up in the world, and she also felt better because she knew she could count on him.

Lucas appeared with a scowl on his face and his fists clenched at the sight of her with another man, laughing and even hugging him.

He was inside chatting to his cousins and couldn't help but notice it had been a while since he last saw her and Montana was nowhere to be found. Part of him felt guilty because he was deliberately avoiding her, trying to get her to come and apologise to him.

It didn't help his temper that Patrizia was still buzzing around him like a pesky gnat and he finally reached the end of this tether, telling her in no uncertain terms they would never be an item.

"Look, its never going to happen. I don't like you. I don't want you. Go and find someone else to annoy," he snapped.

"I don't know what I ever saw in you," she said, furious.

"I do. Money. That's it. Nothing else."

"Well, at least I'm not the one who's chasing and mooning after some poor and inappropriate woman with no class *and* who can't even be bothered to visit your grandfather."

Her words struck a nerve but he was too angry to reply and stalked off. Now as he scanned the crowd, he couldn't believe his eyes when saw Montana standing outside flirting and throwing herself at some guy he didn't recognise on the patio. Anger was once again beginning to rise inside him and he discreetly asked his cousins if they knew who she was talking to but they didn't.

As he approached, he heard them mention James and the fact Lucas wouldn't take it well. His simmering anger was now boiling ready to erupt.

"Montana, who's your *friend*?" he said, through clenched teeth.

"Lucas," she said, looking guilty. "This is Stephen Dobson, he's —"

"About to leave, weren't you Mr Dobson," he said, his voice cold as ice.

Stephen arched an eyebrow at Montana and she nodded.

"It's okay, Steve. It was really good to see you again."

She didn't care Lucas was standing there glaring, she still gave him a hug and a kiss and Stephen muttered good luck to her before moving away.

"What the hell do you call that?" he snapped.

"What?" She had done nothing wrong and refused to feel guilty about it.

"You. Flirting and throwing yourself at some other guy. Do you think making a fool of me will make me jealous?"

"What?" she said, bewildered by his attack before realising his train of thought. "No, you have it all wrong."

"You think *this* is more important than spending time with your best friends."

"What are you talking about?" she said, confused. Maybe he had too much to drink.

"Is he the next sucker you have lined up? Maybe I should just tell him not to expect much from you except in bed."

"What are you talking about? Stephen is my —"

"What about James, Montana? When were you going to tell me about James?"

He sounded so cold and the shock that he knew about James stunned her.

"H-how did you find out?" she whispered, afraid.

"That you love James? You talk in your sleep. I ignored it because the sex was phenomenal, but I see now that's all you were offering — nothing else. Since I'm the man of the moment, maybe I should avail myself of your services, right now."

His mouth came down on hers, punishing her, ravaging her, making her lips bruised. He pushed her into a dark corner so no one could see and pushed her dress up before plunging two fingers into her wetness.

She didn't care even though she felt ashamed of how her body was betraying her and couldn't help but want Lucas as he played and teased her until she cried out into his mouth. Angry at how excited she made him even now, he thrust into her and she could only sob in ecstasy clinging to him as she came over and over driving him over the edge.

Now he was torn between knowing this was the most exciting and daring thing he had ever done — knowing it could only be like this with Montana and knowing she felt it too — and disgusted with himself at how he lost control and brutally took her. As he tidied himself up, he left her with tears rolling silently down her cheeks as she stayed hidden in the shadows.

Lucas was wound tight. He wanted to find Stephen Dobson and tell him in no uncertain terms he would never have Montana before punching his lights out. Then he would find this James guy and tell him he didn't deserve Montana if he couldn't even keep her close to him, but after what he just did, he knew he didn't deserve her either.

"Have you seen Montana?" Isabella and Toni said, looking around for her.

"No," he said, wanting to protect her and give her time to compose herself.

She came in through the doors looking miserable and pale. She was looking around and looked right through them as she scanned the crowd.

He watched her finding her prey and as she headed towards Stephen Dobson, his fists clenched. She whispered something to him and he nodded putting an arm around her and leading her to the door.

Lucas was dammed if he was going to chase after her like a lovesick schoolboy. He wasn't jealous of any man and if she thought Stephen Dobson was a better bet then good on her. He didn't care.

"Who's that she's with?" Toni said, finally spotting her.

"Stephen Dobson." He tried to sound bored, but his gut clenched tightly and his anger was hanging by a very thin thread.

"Stephen Dobson? Oh!" Recognition struck Toni like lightning as Tonio came over and just wanted to know whom she was ogling making her giggle at Tonio's jealousy.

"Steve, but I'm not ogling him. In fact he's…" She stopped her train of thought after Izzy gave her a nudge and a stern look of warning. "A brother of a friend," she lamely said.

Toni might as well hit him over the head with a great big shovel at her words.

"Stephen Dobson is a brother of a friend?" he said, sceptical.

"Yes," Toni frowned. "Didn't Mon introduce you to him?"

"No, she must have forgotten, she's been a bit tired and forgetful lately," he said, trying to cover up his anger that even her friends seemed to have the wool pulled over their eyes.

"Are you sure she's not pregnant?" someone teased, and he blinked at their words.

"Well it wouldn't be mine, it's probably James'," he mocked, and he heard two feminine gasps and knew instantly he said something wrong.

"What did you say?" Izzy said, furious and he was starting to sweat.

"It must be James'." He doubled down.

"Who's James?" Tonio said, confused.

"Montana's other lover," Lucas shrugged.

"You complete and utter jerk!" Izzy raged, as Marco tried to calm his fiancée down. "Don't you dare tell me to calm down, Marco." Unleashing her anger back to Lucas, Izzy said, "I hope for your sake you didn't say something stupid like that to her. I'll *never* forgive you if you've hurt her."

"She's been hurt enough, she doesn't need a jerk like you to twist the knife even more," Toni growled, and ran after Izzy.

The three men were left standing there stunned and bewildered by what just happened.

"Thanks, now we're in the doghouse too. What the hell did you do and what's going on?" Marco said, angry and bewildered.

"I have no idea," Lucas said, shaking his head completely bewildered. "But I'm going to find out."

He followed the women but Stephen and Montana had gone. He tried calling her but she didn't answer, not that he blamed her. He didn't know what exactly he did but felt deep down in his gut, he probably just made the worst mistake of his life.

Chapter Nineteen

"It'll be all right, Mon," Stephen said, trying to comfort a sobbing Montana as he led her to his car.

"No, it won't. I should have told him about James but I was too chicken."

"Where are you staying?"

"At Lucas'."

In that instant, Stephen knew Lucas Romero wasn't just a fling, that he meant more to Montana than that. What he didn't know was just how much more or serious it was.

"Do you want me to drop you there or I can take you back to my hotel or wherever you want."

"Can we go and get my stuff first and I'll move to your hotel for tonight at least," she said, wiping her eyes.

"Of course."

"You're...you're not angry with me, are you?"

The question took him by surprise.

"Why would I be angry?"

"Because I…" She didn't know how to say that she was moving on and that included sleeping with some other man who wasn't James.

"Mon," he said, holding her hand. "No one expects or wants you to hide away from the world and stop living, or to eternally mourn James. We all want you to be happy. Nothing can bring James back. At least while he was here, he had you and was the happiest he had ever been."

She took a deep breath, the worry and guilt inside her slowly dissipating yet the tears still flowing freely.

"Did I ever tell you James and I secretly took an Italian cooking class on Tuesday nights? He wanted to surprise you and figured Italian was easy enough to learn to cook."

The surprised look on her face made him smile as she then shook her head at her husband's subterfuge. Never once had she guessed he hadn't been where he said he was.

"He did? But Tuesdays he always went to the gym."

"I know," he laughed. "After the class, James would quickly come to my place, we'd eat the food and then he'd quickly have a shower and go home. Tuesday was always my favourite night of the week, we had some great laughs."

"I always wondered why the gym took so long. He said he did a lot of weights and there was also a lot of waiting for machines to become free. Actually I even accused him of sneaking takeaways because he didn't look like he was losing weight but gaining it," she said. "Although I think at the time I was more grateful he wasn't having an affair to care if he was sneaking food."

They both laughed and then sobered.

"I still miss him so much," he said, and then she felt the guilt sink in.

"Is it wrong to not miss him and think of him as much?" she whispered, worried Stephen would yell at her for being disloyal to James.

"No. Its different for you, Mon. James was my brother. We grew up together, have all these memories. You and he were just starting out on life together. If you had been married for a lot longer, it would probably be a lot different, but you had less than a year together as husband and wife."

Once again, she was crying and Stephen comforted her even though, he too, was in tears.

"We're all grateful James had you and was happy, that's all we ever cared about, Mon. That's why we want you to be just as happy because no one can change what happened. So to see you moving on would make us all happy."

This was the pep talk she needed to hear. To know James' family weren't going to hate her for moving on, that she wasn't betraying them or James, meant the world to her. Unfortunately, her world was also crumbling down around her.

They went back to Lucas' and as she frantically packed her things, a wave seemed to hit her out of nowhere and she called out.

"S-Steve! I-I don't feel so…" She collapsed in his arms and he scooped her up and took her to the hospital.

When she awoke, she was in a hospital bed and started panicking, thrashing around trying to get up and leave.

"Calm down, Mon. Deep breaths. It's okay, I'm right here beside you. You're in the hospital," he said, holding her hand and telling her to shut her eyes and get some sleep.

The doctor came in with news and told Stephen with the assumption they were a couple, that Montana was pregnant, around six weeks.

As he sat beside her sleeping form, Stephen decided it was up to Montana whether to tell the father, whom he assumed was Lucas Romero, or not, but until then he would say nothing.

When she woke once more, she was a lot calmer and Stephen was dozing in the chair beside her.

"S-Steve," she rasped, her throat dry.

"How are you feeling?" He smiled with concern, holding her hand once more.

"Tired. D-do they know what's wrong with me?"

Still feeling a little frail, tears were welling up in her eyes, even though she wasn't quite sure what for.

"Seems you're pregnant and that's probably why you fainted," he said, letting her take it all in. The shock on her face said it all. "Do you want to tell me about it?"

She burst into tears and then blurted out the whole sorry saga and by the end, he could only nod his understanding.

"Do you think your family will hate me?" she sobbed.

"Of course not. They would be happy you're moving on, Mon. Everyone hurt for you, but nothing will bring James back, you know that."

"But it's only been a short amount of time since James died," she whispered, weighed down with heavy guilt.

"It will be okay," he said. "So now what? No one knows you're here, Mon. I'll help you in any way I can, but if I was Lucas, I'd want to know."

He confirmed what she already knew she would have to do, but she was scared.

"I know," she said, defeated and Stephen's heart ached for her as he sat on the bed and hugged her.

"Do you want me to tell him that you're here?" he said, and she could only nod. "What about the rest? I'm happy to do it or at least give him the reassurance that it's his baby because he's going to think that it's James' baby, Mon."

"I know. I shouldn't be a chicken and get you to do my dirty work, but could you kind of at least explain James is dead or whatever you need to. I can fill the rest in."

"What are brother-in-law's for? Are you sure?" He searched her face to make sure that this was really what she wanted.

"Yes, I'll be fine. I have to grow up sometime, right?" She gave him a small smile and he hugged her.

Lucas looked terrible. When he went home after the party and found all of Montana's things packed and yet still there, it gave him some hope she hadn't left, but she was nowhere to be found.

He waited up until he couldn't keep his eyes open but even then, he couldn't really sleep because it hurt so much and his bedroom felt like it was just an empty shell.

Stupidly, he thought for sure the next day, she would have at least returned for her stuff and then he could apologise, but she never did. So he got blindingly drunk and refused to take any calls. Even when Tonio and Marco turned up on his doorstep, he told them to get lost.

Going to work wasn't any better either. He snapped at everyone and when his PA announced Stephen Dobson was here to see him, he just sank back in his chair ready to be pummelled. He deserved it.

"Good, you look terrible." Stephen smiled as he strode into Lucas' office.

"What do you want?" he snapped, just seeing the man's smug face made him irritated.

"Do you love her?" Stephen wasn't going to beat around the bush, and was grateful it wasn't him in the hot seat.

"Does it really matter now?" he sighed. "I'm probably the biggest idiot on the planet but yes, I do."

Lucas was resigned to knowing that his fate with or without Montana was that he loved her.

"Then I'm here to give you another chance." Stephen was enjoying himself. He never wanted to be in the position Lucas was in and God willing, he never would be.

"Huh?" Lucas was confused. Hadn't Montana left him for good?

"What exactly do you know about Montana?"

"I'm not sure what you're getting at?"

"Do you know her…surname, for instance?"

Although it was a very basic question, Stephen wasn't sure if Montana changed her surname to Dobson or not, knowing that sometimes James would tease Montana about not wanting to join the Dobson clan because she was still a Chan. Surely if she had and Lucas knew it, then wouldn't he have twigged that she and Stephen shared the same surname or perhaps he just was oblivious.

"Actually I can't remember." Lucas heaved a sigh. He wasn't even going to pretend.

Even though he was unsure of what Lucas' answer would be, his answer was even more shocking than Stephen imagined.

"What exactly *do* you know about her?" Another heavy sigh sounded. "How long have you two even *known* each other?" he said, incredulous. "What on earth did you two talk about? Or should that be, you didn't."

Lucas should be angry at this man's judgmental tone but couldn't be.

"Seriously, I'm not here to judge," Stephen said.

Could've fooled him, Lucas thought.

"You're probably aware by now that I'm Montana's *friend*. Or you could possibly even say, like her *brother*."

"Well, at least I can refute that. I know that Montana has two brothers and *neither* are called Stephen," Lucas said, feeling more confident he at least knew *something* about Montana.

"Well, that's something I guess. Then let me give you some advice. Montana is a *very* complex, but loving woman.

She's had things happen in her life no one should have to go through, but she's a survivor."

"I have no idea what the hell you're talking about. Where is she?" Panic mixed with anger was starting to make itself known.

"Hospital. She fainted Saturday night and I took her to the hospital."

"But she hates hospitals." He sagged, all the anger instantly draining away leaving only worry.

"Yes, but do you know why?"

"No, I never bothered to ask." He ruefully shook his head when a light bulb flashed in his mind. "*James.*"

"James." Stephen nodded.

"Is-is she okay?"

"Perfectly fine. They *both* are so if I was you, I'd get my knee pads ready for some serious grovelling." Stephen couldn't help but smirk at Lucas' face.

"Both?" Lucas looked completely dazed.

"Hm, it seems that Montana's pregnant. Six or so weeks. *And* before you jump to the wrong conclusion, *again*, it's yours." Stephen happily said.

"But James…"

"Is dead."

"Dead?"

"Dead."

"When?"

"Just over two years ago. So as you can see, there's no chance it's his. Well, my work here is done. I'll look forward to my wedding invite. Good luck." Stephen smiled, leaving a stunned Lucas sitting there in his office.

A bright smile slowly stole across his face and he rushed out the door telling his PA he wouldn't be back today. Montana was going to have his baby. The thought shone through him as he raced to the hospital but when he got there, she was gone.

He raced home and saw all her stuff was also now gone. No one could tell him where she went and suddenly he had fallen into a black hole.

Lucas pestered Izzy and Toni for Montana's whereabouts, but they either both knew and refused to tell him or they truly didn't know. However, as close as the women were, he highly suspected it was the former rather than the latter and they thought they were doing the right thing by protecting Montana from him. He also tried to get them to tell him about James, but they refused to budge on that topic too, saying it wasn't their place to tell him.

All he knew was Montana was having his baby and he couldn't find her. Never had he felt so lost in his life and knowing there was no one to blame but himself and this whole mess was all his own stupid jealous fault. Hadn't Montana taught him that being open and upfront saved a world of misunderstandings? And yet, he hadn't done that. He had sulked, pouted and been jealous, but not once asked her who James was. If he had, all this could have been avoided and they both could have been celebrating such wonderful news together.

Admittedly, he never told anyone Montana was supposedly pregnant with his child. He needed to find her to sort it all out before announcing to the world he was about to become a father.

What if she aborted it? Even the thought stabbed at his heart, but there was a flicker of hope deep down that knew she wouldn't do that. Even if she hated him with every fibre of her being, she wouldn't abort their child. He clung hard to that hope because it was all he had right now.

Sitting feeling helpless, he realised just how little he knew about her. It was as Stephen Dobson said, he never even really took the time to get to know her or her life, he just dragged her along with his. No wonder she easily disappeared.

Remorse and regret overcame him and he filled the void with work and more work.

Chapter Twenty

All Montana ever wanted was to be a wife and mother. She wasn't a woman who wanted a high-flying corporate job or even to be wealthy, she just wanted the simple things which to some people would be considered boring or even outdated.

Finding out she was pregnant with Lucas' baby overwhelmed her with happiness until she grounded herself in the reality of knowing they weren't together, which made her miserable.

The good news was Indi was en route to London to start her OE and Montana couldn't have been more relieved to have her sister for support.

"Indi!" she cried, finally being able to hold and see her sister in the flesh at the airport. "I'm so glad that you're here."

"Me too, Mon. I've missed you so much."

"Me too."

They were still hugging and crying sure that everyone was looking but they didn't care. It had been too long since they were together.

"I can't wait to meet this hunk of yours and Izzy's and Toni's of course. Do you think they have another spare cousin or brother for me?" Indi teased.

Montana's heart sank. How was she supposed to tell her sister that although Indi's arrival was perfect timing, her own life was a big, fat mess.

"I'm just glad you finally made it. Let's go home and I'll fill you in on all the comings and goings."

Indi could sense something was making her sister miserable and seeing as the Tube wasn't the place to discuss it, she distracted them both by discussing what she should see and do in London and the rest of the UK and Europe.

"All right, spill it," Indi said, as soon as she settled in.

"Spill what?"

"Whatever has you down in the dumps."

"I can't get anything past you, can I?"

"No, but only because I'm standing in front of you and can tell something's wrong."

"So as you know I was recently in Italy to celebrate Izzy's engagement party," she said.

"Yes, how did it go?" Indi was excited to hear all the gossip.

"It was *huge* and totally extravagant. I hadn't realised just how wealthy the Romeros are," she smiled. "Then Lucas asked me to stay for another week as the following weekend, his eldest sister, Giana was having a celebration for her new baby."

"Did the ba—he cheat on you?" Indi said, stopping herself from swearing just in time after seeing the sadness on her sister's face.

"N-No, nothing like that. It was great until his grandfather had a heart attack and I-I couldn't even go into the hospital," she sobbed.

"Oh no. Oh, Mon. It's okay." Indi held her sister tightly now. God, it must have been absolutely terrifying for her, she thought to herself.

Indi vividly remembered the day James died. She had been at home and answered the phone and all she could hear was Montana's sobbing down the line. She wasn't making much sense, but the words James and hospital were all that seemed coherent. Taking over the conversation so Montana only needed to grunt answers, Indi managed to piece together James was at the hospital and it was an emergency. She quickly rushed around and told the family.

They drove like crazy people to get to there to support her and while their parents comforted Montana, Indi took her sister's cell phone to call James' family for her. It was the worst phone call she ever had to make, telling someone's family their loved one was in the hospital. They too, were in a state of shock.

The Dobson family arrived still unable to comprehend what was happening when a doctor came to tell them James had died a few minutes earlier from a massive heart attack.

Seeing everyone collapse from the anguish was one of the most horrific moments of her life and Indi's heart hurt for her sister, and even now she was full of compassion and empathy.

"We fought about it and I couldn't even explain to him about James, I was such a coward."

"No, Mon. You're not a coward. Even I have trouble with seeing hospitals, even TV hospital dramas because of what happened. You were upset and overwhelmed and he was too busy worrying about his grandfather to take the time to listen. It was just bad timing, that's all. It's no one's fault," Indi said, as Montana gave her sister a grateful smile.

She hadn't thought of it like that at all. All she could think was that Lucas hadn't been understanding, and while she understood he had been worried about his grandfather, but what about afterwards? Why hadn't he cared enough then to find out the truth from her?

"But he didn't want to know later on."

"Well, maybe he is just an idiot then," Indi said.

It made Montana feel so much better knowing her sister was on her side.

"What I didn't know was that somewhere along the line, I talked in my sleep and said I love James."

"Oh no," Indi gasped.

"Yes, so Lucas thought I had some other man, and it all came to a head at the Romero family shindig where I ran into Steve, James' brother. Lucas totally got the wrong end of the stick and confronted me about James."

Indi's hand flew to her mouth at her sister's words. It was like seeing a train crash happening right before your eyes. You knew it was going to happen, but there was nothing you could do to stop it.

"Steve took me back to Lucas' where I packed to leave but I fainted and ended up in hospital. I know, freaky right, but actually being inside it wasn't as bad as walking through the doors," she said. "The chicken that I am, I left it up to Steve to tell Lucas where I was and about…the baby," Montana quietly said, waiting for her sister's reaction.

"B-Baby?" Indi's eyes were wide as saucers.

After Montana finished telling Indi her story and all the tears fell, Indi was not only supportive but ecstatic.

"You can't tell *anyone*, Inds," she said. "You know the family will freak out, especially mum and dad and I don't need a lecture from the other side of the world since Lucas and I aren't together either."

"I promise," Indi said. "What about Lucas? Surely he's going to turn up here looking for you?"

"What for?" she said, miserable. "Even if Steve tells him the truth, he probably wouldn't believe it. I should have told him about James, but I just couldn't."

"Then he's an idiot and you're better off without him."

Montana appreciated Indi's unwavering support. It was just what she needed.

"Don't be too hard on him, Inds, its not like we were ever in a real relationship. We never talked about anything other than superficial things or work, or we had sex."

Once again Indi's eyes were wide.

"*You* were having a *fling*?"

Montana wanted to laugh at her sister's shock.

"I know, its not like me but if you ever meet Lucas, you'll see why."

"Then he's a moronic idiot for not realising just how awesome you are out of bed as well and getting to know that side of you."

"Thanks, Inds. I'm so glad that you're here."

Indi hugged her sister and then they began to make plans for her stay.

Montana had a doctor's appointment and Indi offered to join her.

"Do you want me to come with you?"

"No, I'll be okay."

Hearing the sadness in Montana's voice, Indi knew her sister was lying, but still she respected her wishes.

"Are you sure?"

"Yes."

As much as she wanted Indi there it would also make her feel even more miserable because Lucas wasn't.

"Young lady, you and your baby are fine. Just keep up your routine, eating well, exercising and getting some rest," Dr Conrad smiled.

She smiled at the use of his 'young lady'. The doctor didn't look any older than her and as she looked at how handsome he was, once upon a time her heart would have done a rat-a-tat-tat but ever since Lucas, there was nothing.

"Okay, Doc," she said.

"Good. Now just to make sure you understand, I mean no free-diving, bungy jumping or skydiving? The poor baby won't know what's happening if you did," Dr Conrad teased.

"Darn it," she smiled. "Guess I better cancel the hotdog eating contest too."

"I love a reasonable patient," he chuckled.

"Thank you."

Heading home, Montana found herself needing a quiet moment to process everything that was going on and was about to happen in her life.

Wandering into the place she always thought was just a park, she realised she was actually on the grounds of a Buddhist temple. Worried she was trespassing on private property, her fears were allayed when she saw there were a lot of people either just sitting with their thoughts, meditating, or also walking and enjoying their solitude. Some were even doing gentle exercising in a small group or reading under the trees on a bench.

Silently agreeing with these strangers that sitting in amongst the trees would not only be calming but also relaxing, Montana let the tranquillity of the place surround her. Finding an empty bench to sit on she sat and thought about how her life had changed so dramatically. Although she still missed James, she knew none of this would have happened if he hadn't died, and felt a twinge of guilt the pain of losing him was lessening. Seeing James' brother, Stephen also relieved her of a huge amount of guilt that was also weighing her down.

Sighing, her thoughts turned to Lucas and how she missed everything about him. His arrogance, his charming personality, his face, smile, eyes, his warmth and humour — everything — because he now owned her heart, broken and all.

Unsure how long she sat there just thinking, she now felt she could put all her jumbled emotions and thoughts into some sort of order and was ready to face whatever the future held.

Gianni Romero was finally out of the hospital and his entire family were constantly fussing over him, which made him feel very smothered, yet very loved. He also heard all the whispers when no one thought he was listening and wasn't sure what to make of them, so he decided it was time to have a chat with his grandson.

"How are you nonno?" Lucas said, as they sat outside enjoying the sunshine and having a little lunch.

"Fine. All this fussing is making me want to be stronger and healthier by the day so that they'll stop."

"Then its working," he laughed.

"Now tell me, what's all this I hear about you and this lovely woman."

Trust his grandfather to get to the heart of the matter.

"It's a *long* story," he sighed.

"Well, its not like I've got anything else to do and it'll at least give me some sort of distraction for a while."

"It'll do that," Lucas said, retelling his story.

"You're an idiot," Gianni said, when Lucas finished.

"That I am."

"Why didn't you just ask her?"

"Because I didn't want to know the truth — good or bad." He shook his head at his own stupidity.

"So you just let her believe you think she's got some sort of other boyfriend?"

"She ran off before we could talk about it," he said, petulant.

"Do you blame her? I don't," Gianni said.

Lucas still felt guilty over the way he treated Montana at the party. He had been a brute using her like that and the shame and guilt would always be with him.

"Do you believe this man who came to tell you Montana's story?" Gianni was only asking to see if Lucas realised the truth of his feelings towards Montana yet.

"Of course. It's too elaborate to be some kind of lie or scam."

"Then don't you think it's time to own up to your feelings about her?"

"It's pretty obvious I like her, nonno. I mean I wouldn't have kept wanting to spend time with her if I didn't."

"Lucas, you are an idiot," Gianni sighed. "Just admit you love her, then go find and marry her, have lots of little bambinos and be happy."

It was on the tip of Lucas' tongue to say that's what he wanted to do but couldn't find her, instead he sat there like a sulky schoolboy.

"What? I don't love her, nonno. I don't even know her that well." He might have told Stephen Dobson he did, but after discovering Montana left him, he reverted back to being in denial about it.

"Fine, then marry Patrizia Rossi. Word has it you have an *understanding* and she's very family orientated and wants you. After all, she did come and visit me regularly in the hospital whereas this woman you're miserable about didn't even bother to show her face."

Good grief, did everybody in his family know about Patrizia and her lies?

"We don't have an *understanding*. She, Pia and Allegra made that up to not only cause mischief but to try and send Mon packing. Thankfully, Mon isn't that stupid and you can be sure I definitely won't be marrying Patrizia *ever*."

This was news to Gianni ears. He might love his granddaughters, one who was named after his wife, but he didn't like their manipulating ways.

"Do tell? Why didn't Montana not believe them?" Now he was even more curious about the woman Lucas loved, even though he already knew her version.

"It started when she came over to tell me of the 'run-in' she had with the three of them, where she was told of this *understanding*," he chuckled, remembering that night.

"I think it was the first time in my life a woman has ever been so upfront and honest about other women being jealous and catty. Believe me, we were all in shock. She knew the game they were playing and just thought she'd bring it to my attention and wasn't even upset as such, more matter of fact, I guess you'd say," he said, his voice full of respect.

"I asked her about it. Why she'd tell me and her friends if she didn't believe it. Mon said it was because of her family, there have always been devious and sly tricks and manipulations her siblings tried over the years, along with friends, that she found the best way to deal with such people and information was to just put it out in the open. Defuse any kind of *misunderstanding* if you will."

He could see his grandfather looking thoughtful, trying to make sense of his explanation.

"Mon could see Patrizia's jealousy a mile away and wanted to make sure that if I wanted Patrizia, I only had to say the word and she'd step aside. If she hadn't said a word then I'd be none the wiser about what those three were up to. Even Marco was shocked his sisters would act like that. I guess because of Mon telling me what Patrizia was up to, then she could believe me when I told her I wasn't interested and never would be in Patrizia."

"I see. This Montana sounds like a very open and honest person. Tell me, why did she not come to the hospital to visit?" Gianni asked the question lightly, not to make Lucas feel guilty because Gianni already guessed the reason, but he wanted to know if Lucas understood.

"I don't know. I never asked her. I was worried for you and when she said she wouldn't come in I got annoyed and left her outside. After that we called a truce, I agreed she wouldn't have to come to the hospital and meet you. I did try one last time but she stubbornly refused."

"And still, you didn't bother to ask her for a reason."

"No." He looked ashamed and guilty once more. "Now she's disappeared and I don't know where to find her."

"Why would she leave?" Gianni said.

"We had words. She said she loved another man in her sleep, nonno," he said, defensive. "So I accused her of cheating on me." And worse, he thought, but wisely kept silent about what an even bigger idiot he had been.

"I see," Gianni said, thoughtful. "So you didn't talk about why she would have said another man's name?"

"We had words, angry words and then she just disappeared," he said, miserable. "I just can't believe she just left."

"You can't? Would you not feel the same way she probably does if you said you loved another woman in your sleep and weren't even asked for an explanation?"

Gianni was wondering if his normally level-headed, sensible grandson truly was an idiot. Nothing he heard so far painted Lucas in any kind of favourable light. He was wondering if he should mention he had met Montana, but decided to leave it for now.

"If it had been an innocent explanation, then she would have stuck around and told me." Again, he sat there sulking like a child, exasperating his grandfather.

"You've just told me how open and honest she is. Don't you think if you bothered to ask her, she would have told you the truth? For all you knew, it could have been her dog's name."

Lucas remained silent because his guilt was eating away at him. His nonno was right and he didn't want to admit it.

"Can I tell you a story about a lovely young woman I met? In fact, she was the one who thought I might have been having a heart attack even when I thought I wasn't," Gianni said. "We were sharing life stories since both of us have lost loved ones. Unfortunately while I had a long and happy life with your nonna, she lost hers very young and quickly. Now she was trying to figure out how to move on with her life without feeling guilty."

Lucas had no idea why his grandfather was telling him all this, but since he was still recovering, he humoured him.

"Although she didn't know me, she still sent flowers, and between you and me, they were the most cheerful ones I got. Every time I saw them I smiled."

Was his grandfather saying he had crush on this mysterious woman? Then a dreaded thought hit that he might want Lucas to find her for him.

"That's great nonno, but I don't understand…"

Gianni sighed. No, Lucas wouldn't understand, he was too busy wallowing to join the very loose dots together, so he decided to just be blunt.

"Do you love Montana, Lucas? I mean, really truly, love her like I love your nonna."

"I don't know." He blew out a breath and raked a hand through his hair.

The action brought Gianni's sharp eyes to focus on the dishevelled state of his grandson, something he hadn't noticed earlier. Lucas looked tired and less than immaculate in his dress, something that wasn't usual.

"Yes. Yes I do." He couldn't deny it any longer.

"Maybe you need to go to her house and see if she's there," Gianni said.

"Go to New Zealand?"

"She lives in New Zealand? She came all this way just for Marco's engagement party?" Now Gianni was confused, he thought Montana said she lived in London.

"No, she and Toni live in London. In fact, Toni's moved over to Italy to be with Tonio."

That news made Gianni brightly smile. He truly liked the women his grandsons found. They were all perfect matches.

"Oh." The lightbulb went on in Lucas' brain. Somehow in all the misery and guilt he completely forgot Montana lived in London. For some reason he thought she was in New Zealand. It would be a lot easier to go to London and see if she were there. "Thanks nonno. I think my head's finally screwed back on and thinking straight."

"If you love her, don't come back without her," Gianni said, silently praying Lucas would be able to make up for all the stupidity he had shown and Montana would be forgiving and give his idiotic grandson another chance.

Chapter Twenty-one

While Montana was out, Indi was trying to make plans on what to do and see in Europe. She didn't seem to love London as much as she thought she would and decided she'd stay long enough to see everything she wanted while making sure her sister had the support she needed.

There was a knock at the door and upon opening it she saw a hunky man standing before her.

"Hi, can I help you?"

"Ah…is Montana here?"

The man looked not only nervous but a whole lot like the Lucas her sister had shown her photos of. Suppressing an enthusiastic yet annoyed welcome that he finally came for Montana, she decided to enact a little mischief and teach him a lesson.

"No. No Montanas here. You must have the wrong place. Sorry."

She shut the door smiling to herself, wondering if Lucas was going to knock again or if he was going to walk away.

Lucas raked a hand through his hair. He was sure Tonio gave him the correct address and yet the woman standing in front of him definitely wasn't Montana.

He turned to walk away and then a thought hit. Did the woman who just answered the door look similar to Montana and did she also have a Kiwi accent? He wasn't sure if he was just wishing for similarities or if they were real.

Standing there debating what he would say if he knocked on the door again, he turned and knocked.

Indi smiled at the knock, glad Lucas wasn't one to give up so easily. While there had been a pause, she thought about what she was going to say to him if he did indeed return, only she hadn't expected it quite so soon.

"Yes?" she said, trying hard not to smile or even confess who she was or where Montana was, as a sense of excitement now hummed through her.

Lucas studied the woman's face carefully and strained to catch her accent but it was hard from her one word answer, he was going to have to wing this and also try to get her to talk more.

"Indiana, right?" he said, hesitant.

"Sorry?"

"You're Indiana…Indi for short. Montana's sister?"

"And you are?"

Relief flooded through him that although she hadn't confirmed it, she also hadn't denied it either, making him suspect he was right on the money. This beautiful woman standing in front of him was Montana's younger sister.

"Lucas. Lucas Romero. I'm Montana's…boyfriend," he said, hoping she'd buy his little white lie. He wasn't sure what Montana had told her family about him, or if she'd mentioned him at all, and that just made him frown some more.

Indi gave Lucas a silent clap for at least working out she was not only Montana's sister, but which one and even knew her name. But that wasn't enough to let him off the hook.

"Hmm, Mon didn't tell me she was seeing anyone…" She frowned, enjoying making Lucas squirm and judging by the crestfallen look on his face, clearly she was naturally talented in the acting department. "Let alone have a boyfriend."

"I swear, we're dating."

"Like I said, she hasn't mentioned a boyfriend at all. How do I know you're not some kind of stalker trying to fool me?"

He looked horrified by the accusation and she wondered just how long she could string him along. This was so much fun.

"I'm not a *stalker*," he said, raking a hand through his hair. "Look, my cousins and I met Mon and her friends on San Miguel. Her best friend, Izzy is now engaged to my cousin, Marco and her other best friend, Toni is totally in love with my other cousin, Antonio."

"So? You're trying to pressure my sister into having some kind of fling with you just because her friends and your cousins have hooked up? What are you, some kind of arrogant jerk who thinks my sister would be so desperate now her friends have partners, that she'd just take the first guy to show her some interest? And besides, what's wrong with you that you can't get your own girlfriend? Are you too lazy to even make an effort with a woman?"

Lucas begrudgingly admitted Indi was a great guard dog for Montana. She wasn't about to give him an inch and if he wanted to know where Montana was, he was going to have to not only work for it, but also win over Indiana in the process.

"Look, I'm here to see Montana. Can you please tell me where she is or when she'll be back?"

"Interesting," she said, tapping her finger to her lips. "You say you know my sister, are even her boyfriend, and yet you turn up here unannounced looking for her. Why haven't you even tried calling her to find out her whereabouts? Sorry dude, but I think you're lying."

"Wait!" he panicked, holding the door so Indi couldn't shut it on him. "I have tried calling but she's obviously screening my calls, that's why I came here. *Please*, can you help me?"

"And that should give you a *huge* clue she wants nothing to do with you. Be a man and take a hint. Or even better, why don't you go and finish your *understanding* with Patrizia." Her tone brooked no further discussion as she shut the door, smiling to herself.

Good grief, he sighed to himself. Who else knew about this stupid understanding with Patrizia and would keep throwing it in his face like it was all his fault when he had nothing to do with it? Now what was he going to do? Montana's sister was a huge obstacle to overcome and yet, he was pleased she had Indi for support.

Leaving, he knew he was going to have to find another way around Indi if he was going to get to Montana.

Montana returned home more relaxed and yet still torn between happy the baby was healthy and miserable because Lucas wasn't here to share all these exciting things with her and she missed him.

"So how did it go?" Indi said, unable to contain her smile.

"Great. All is fine. What's got you in such a good mood?" Montana hoped it was something good because she could use some cheering up.

"Oh, nothing. I just had a visitor."

"Who was it?"

"Oh, no one you'd know," Indi fibbed. "Wrong door."

"And that makes you happy?"

"Well, he was a hunk."

"Lucas is a hunk," Montana said, under her breath.

"What's that?"

"Nothing."

"So when are you going to tell Lucas about the baby?"

"I think Stephen already has."

"And?"

"And what? You know I skedaddled as fast as I could."

"I can't believe that *you* of all people are such a chicken."

"I am not *a chicken*," Montana huffed.

"Sure you're not," Indi drawled. "You got someone else to do your dirty work for you and then ran as fast as possible. Mon, you know that's not like you. You're usually direct and upfront, *no hiding. It's the Chan sibling way.*"

Normally those words would make them all laugh and smile since they all agreed that as siblings they were very forthright, but it seemed Montana wasn't in the mood for a little teasing.

"Well, I didn't want to see Lucas' reaction."

"*And* didn't you tell me that you told him about Patrizia's *understanding*? So if you can do that, why can't you just confront him and either tell him he's a jerk and you want nothing more to do with him unless it's baby-related, or that you're stubborn but love him."

They both could sense Montana's fears so Indi eased up and hugged her sister.

"As mum would say, 'it'll all work itself out in the end'," Indi said.

"I thought it was, 'it'll all come out in the wash'?"

"Either way, it'll all work out."

They both sat there silently praying it would.

Lucas returned to Montana's determined to see her and he wasn't leaving until he had.

"Oh, you again," Indi said, answering the door yet secretly she was pleased not only had Lucas returned, but this time he looked like a man with a plan. Too bad she was about to ruin it.

"Is Montana here?"

"Actually she's not."

"How do I know you're not lying?" he said. "Mon! Mon!"

"You can stop shouting. I told you, Mon's not here."

"Then where is she?" He raked a hand through his hair.

"She's gone to the last place you'd ever look for her, or perhaps, it's the first."

Seeing how her cryptic answer confused and irritated him, she couldn't help but smile.

"Come on, Indi, *please*, I'm begging. Where is Mon?"

"If I tell you, you owe me a two or three month *all expenses paid* holiday around Europe so I can say I've seen everything that needs to be seen and can go home happy."

"You're not staying?" Her words stunned him.

"No. In the very short time I've been here to visit and spend time with my sister, not only has that not really happened, but I've decided London really isn't my scene."

"But what if she needs your…support?" He tried to diplomatically ask the question without actually referring to Montana's pregnancy because he wasn't sure if Indi knew about it or not, and didn't want to be the one to let the cat out of the bag, even by accident.

"I'm sure that once you've sorted out what a gigantic jackass you've been, done a lot of grovelling and apologised and Mon's forgiven you, then she won't need my support. She'll have you and your sisters, who by the way, sound lovely."

Lucas couldn't believe Indi was being so supportive when she didn't even know him or his family.

"You'd actually like Sofia, you remind me of her," he smiled.

"Well, I could use a travel buddy so if she's got nothing better to do then I'm sure we'll have a great time."

"I'll let her know, but Indi, I thought all Kiwis did the *big* OE, you know, that right of passage thing?"

"I've decided Canada's the country for me so I'll tour around Europe and get my fill and then return home and see if I can get a Canadian working visa. I just wanted to be sure I wasn't a London girl first, and it looks like I'm not."

To her surprise, he hugged her.

"What was that for?"

"For being Mon's sister and caring."

"I'm still not telling you where she went. If you love her like you say, then you'll have to put the effort in to get her back."

He scribbled a number down on a piece of paper and handed it to her.

"What's this?"

"Sofia's number. I'll tell her to expect your call, I'm sure she'll be up for a little adventure, especially if it's on me," he chuckled. "Now I have to go and find my future wife."

He hugged her one last time and she found herself relenting and taking pity on him.

"Go back to the beginning."

"Go back to the beginning?" he said, confused.

"That's all I'm saying and good luck. I can't go on my travels until you guys get back together so make it quick."

He laughed and departed deep in thought trying to work out where the beginning was. Then just like that his face lit up and he beamed. He knew exactly where his future wife and mother of his child was. Now he had plans to make.

Chapter Twenty-two

The gentle breeze enveloped Montana as she looked out over what had earlier been crystal clear blue water, which was now a darker sapphire colour due to the time. The sun was descending on San Miguel and the sky slowly changed from blue to dusky pinks and deep oranges. Four whole days of bliss and total relaxation. Timeout in a place where she was free and alone to gather her thoughts and not have to worry about anything.

After tonight it would all be over.

Back to reality.

It was Indi who encouraged her to take time out and relax. To try and decide what to do next with her life, Lucas and the baby.

Although she agreed with Indi, she hadn't planned on coming back to where it all began. It was Indi's take charge bossiness that somehow had her booking a ticket and then winging her way back to the paradise of San Miguel.

In the first few days she spent a lot of time reminiscing about James and their brief life together, shedding a lot of tears knowing she would forever treasure that part of her life, but he was no longer here and it was time to let him go and be at peace. Seeing Stephen again also helped to ease the burden of guilt she felt.

She also spent a lot of time thinking about Lucas. How much she loved him and then how miserable she felt, at how much she missed him.

The thought of having a baby — Lucas' baby — made her happy and sad at the same time. Would he be a part of its life? Would he want to be? Could they be a family unit or would they end up having a child that was shuttled between its parents? If she and Lucas didn't get back together, would she go back and live in New Zealand with her family around her or should she try and stay in Europe, either England or perhaps Italy so their child could be close to Lucas as well?

It was these questions that hurt her head and heart. She never ever once thought of bringing a child into the world that wasn't part of a loving family unit.

Sitting at the table she occupied — more like monopolised — during her stay as the maître d' clearly took pity on her on her first night when he realised she was alone and therefore had given her a lovely table on the terrace overlooking the ocean. Montana was grateful. The wonderful view gave her time to think and reflect. However, tonight was different, tonight was an ending and tomorrow would be her new beginning in the next phase of her life.

Landing on the island, memories instantly came flooding back as soon as Lucas stepped off the plane.

Everywhere he looked, he was reminded of Montana and the last time they were both here. As much as excitement and anticipation filled him that he was finally not only going to see her but also make everything right again, he was also filled with anxiety that perhaps she wouldn't want to try again. After all, he knew he hurt her deeply.

Swatting away the sliver of guilt he felt about lying to his cousins when they talked and planned things, which he subtly evaded committing to, using a fake work trip as an excuse so he could come alone to the place where he met the love of his life, knowing if he told his cousins the truth, then they'd all be here together either trying to help him or protect Montana, or both.

No, this was something he not only needed to do by himself, but he and Montana also needed time alone to sort it out themselves.

The realisation hit like a tsunami pummelling him. He truly, deeply loved Montana. Sure he briefly thought it, had even said it aloud, but knew deep down he still hadn't really acknowledged it — heart and soul. Even his grandfather knew before he had that Montana was the one for him.

God, he was an idiot. No wonder Montana ran away as fast as she could, all because of his own stupidity.

Lucas' senses immediately zoned in on Montana without even looking around the room. She was at the same table she occupied last night, when she had a look of melancholy, like someone just wanting to have some alone time for their thoughts and he didn't have the nerve to approach. Tonight though her body language looked different. She seemed to be sitting taller like the weight of the world was gone and her angelic face glowed as she seemed more relaxed.

He was also glad she hadn't seen him last night. He needed his own time and space to think long and hard about what he wanted for the future, hopefully with her in it. Tonight, he couldn't stay away a moment longer.

"I see you are alone. May I join you?" he said, pulling out the chair and sitting.

Looking amused by the man's confident arrogance she wasn't about to scream blue murder at his intrusion or decline his offer, Montana tried to hide how startled she was Lucas was now in front of her.

"As if I have a choice. So why not?" She dismissively waved her hand. "I should tell you though, that if you're looking for a one-night stand, or heaven forbid a rich woman, you've picked the completely wrong person."

"Then it is good that I'm not looking for any of those things. Just someone to share dinner with me?" he said, highly amused.

"Hmm, interesting" she said, looking around. "You could have sat at any of these tables and yet you chose mine. If looks could kill, I'd say I'd be a disintegrated mess on this chair right now considering half the women in the room are shooting laser beams at me."

"That's because they're just jealous of your beauty and the fact I chose you and not them."

Lucas looked at Montana and noticed the sadness that seemed to be reflected in her brown eyes. Her hair was a luxurious jet black, like silk strands glistening in the light. She wore a simple summer dress but it made her look like she should be in a field picking wildflowers and thinking of her lover and he was getting aroused hoping he was that lover.

"Oh, you're a sweet talker. Tell you what, you pay for your meal, I'll pay for mine and we'll share conversation. So tell me about yourself?"

Still rattled by the fact Lucas was sitting opposite her, Montana decided perhaps she could play pretend for one night. Maybe this would either be a new start or an ending. She didn't know which she wanted. Yes, she did, she just didn't want to admit it to herself.

Looking at the man opposite her, the man who made her heart beat faster just thinking of him but his nearness made it gallop, she still couldn't help but marvel at how handsome he was.

It had to be all the confidence he exuded, never mind the casual designer trousers that looked tailor-made or the crisp white linen shirt that just emphasised his tan all the more. His dark hair looked slightly damp which meant he'd either had a swim or just got out of the shower, but it was his cologne that sent her mind spinning.

Lucas' smell always made her smile and tingle.

With her mind wondering, she didn't even hear him talking to her.

"What? Pardon me, I was miles away. What did you say?" she blushed.

"I was just asking if you have enjoyed your holiday here in San Miguel?"

He noted Montana had zoned out and wasn't sure if that was a good or bad thing. If she was thinking of him or them, that had to be a good thing, otherwise…he wasn't sure if he really wanted to know.

"Oh, *loved* it. It has been the best holiday ever. Just chilling and doing nothing. It's so peaceful and beautiful. And what do you do?"

"Oh, I'm just a simple business man here on business."

"*Right*," she drawled. "I've heard all about you businessmen. All right, Mr Businessman, how would you like to have a bet?"

When he sat down and started talking to Montana, he took it as a chance to start over, but now she wanted to have a bet? His body went taut.

"What kind of bet?" he said, wary.

"If I went to the restroom right now, one of these women in here would be coming up to hit on you as soon as I'm halfway across the room."

"Okay, and if you win? What is it that you want?"

"The loser buys dinner. So how about it?"

"Deal," he smiled.

"Oh, if the waiter comes over can you please tell him I'll have the crispy duck risotto and another ginger ale, thanks."

Lucas watched the graceful movement of her body as the summer dress swished around her long legs. Then he silently groaned that Montana was right, she hadn't even reached the halfway point of her journey before a sleek feminine woman in a tight-fitting yellow dress approached the table and sat down without even being asked.

Not only did he not know her but he found it to be bad manners, especially since he hadn't given this woman even a flicker of interest, in fact he hadn't even realised she was in the room, his eyes were only on Montana.

Still the woman was confident of her success as much as she was trying to encourage him to privately view more of what was on offer.

He politely and firmly managed to get rid of his rather bold visitor, although he wasn't shocked by how forward she was with what she not only said, but advertised. He didn't want what she was offering on a dessert platter.

Miss Yellow dress left the table annoyed Lucas hadn't succumbed to her charms, but he didn't care. The only woman he would ever want was Montana. It had taken him long enough to realise he was in love with her and now that he had, he wasn't about to let her easily get away.

He was enjoying tonight with Montana and was happy to role play if that was what she wanted. Watching her return to the table, the smile on her face seemed to dazzle.

"So, was I right? Did some woman come up to you while I was gone?" she said.

"Yes. I would like to say that you were wrong, but unfortunately you weren't."

"You know you could have had dinner with her instead. I wouldn't have been offended," she said, looking discreetly around the room. "Hmm, was it the woman in the ultra tight yellow dress, by any chance?"

For a fleeting moment Lucas wondered if this had been a set-up. But then realised no, Montana wouldn't do such a thing and besides, she didn't even know he was here on the island until he sat down at her table.

"Again, you are right. Why did you think that the woman who approached me would be the one in the yellow dress?"

"She was the one with the laser beam eyes," she laughed.

His light chuckle made her toes curl but it was his deep yet caressing voice that made her heart beat a little faster.

"I wish to apologise, but I don't think that we've actually introduced ourselves. My manners are not usually this terrible. I am Lucas, and you are?"

"Montana."

"Montana. A beautiful name for a beautiful woman."

"Flatterer," she laughed.

Lucas watched the way Montana laughed and the way it lit up her face just made her seem more beautiful and more *real*.

"So why have you not travelled here with friends?" he said, curious.

"What makes you think I don't have any friends?"

He realised she just caught him in a trap. He couldn't very well tell her he saw her sitting at the same table last night alone.

"Well, wouldn't they be sitting here joining you, instead of me?"

"True."

"So…"

"So?"

"So why are you not here with friends?"

"Didn't want to be." She shrugged.

He hoped perhaps she came back here to remember him and the connection they had.

"Why are you here?" she said, her heart beating rapidly waiting for his answer.

The corners of his mouth curled upwards as the impish twinkle of his eyes once again made her toes curl.

"I thought we already discussed that if I was looking for a rich woman or a one-night stand that I've picked the completely wrong person," he said, repeating her earlier words.

"We did."

"Then, perhaps I've just seen the woman I wish to spend the rest of my life with…my soul mate as you ladies love to say."

Montana had a brief moment of panic at his words. There was a lump in her throat making it hard to swallow. Surely Lucas couldn't possibly, honestly be thinking that they were soul mates. It was cruel to even wish for such a thing.

Dare she hope his words rang true?

Having Lucas here was a dream come true or was that all it was, a dream. She almost pinched herself to see if she was awake or not.

Although he enjoyed seeing her look so discombobulated at his answer, she also looked almost afraid of what he said making him frown. Surely she knew he spoke the truth.

After dinner, he offered to walk her back to her room, she resisted the temptation knowing it wouldn't have ended there.

"How about a walk on the beach instead?" she said.

As disappointed as he was that she was still holding him at arms length, he agreed, hoping to wear her down on their walk.

It was silent. A long drawn out silence and yet neither moved to try and break it which Montana appreciated. There was always an aura of contentment and ease around Lucas and their silences and she was glad they still had it, no matter what issues they were dealing with.

Finally he saw her to her hotel door and gave her a gentle yet lingering kiss goodnight. By all accounts it was chaste, but the emotion that passed through them showed there were unresolved feelings.

"Will you meet me on the beach tomorrow morning?" she said.

The smile that lit up his face at her suggestion made her realise it was a great one.

"If I'm not there —"

"You'll be in the water."

They both smiled at each other.

"Goodnight Mon. Sweet dreams." He gave her another gentle yet passionate kiss, one that brought tears to her eyes and left.

Chapter Twenty-three

The next morning was much like the very first time she ever laid eyes on Lucas.

She was down at the beach but it was still too dark to see if he was out there amongst the waves, yet somehow she could sense he was. They were both in places where their thoughts were their own.

Once again, she found herself thinking of James and the sad smile on her face meant she was finally ready to just let him be a great memory, to be able to let him go and fly free.

"James, I'll always love and miss you," she said, aloud. "I hope you'll be happy for me and know you'll always be in my heart, but I love Lucas now, he's my future, the man I want to spend the rest of my life with."

A gust of wind blew and she wanted to think it was James saying he heard her and was saying goodbye.

She smiled with sadness, tears falling knowing she was finally closing this chapter with James, but there was just something about San Miguel that made everything begin anew and as if Lucas knew she had said her final goodbyes, he emerged from the water beaming and in that instant she knew for certain Lucas was the man she wanted to spend the rest of her life with. James would always have a special place in her heart but Lucas, Lucas was her future.

Montana's idea to meet on the beach to watch the sunrise gave him hope. It was like he was being given a second chance — a do-over — and this time he wasn't going to blow it.

His heart almost stopped when he came out of the water and saw she had been crying, unsure if the tears were because she was about to cut whatever thin thread that held them together or something else.

Now he knew he not only loved her, yet been a terrible jerk to her, he was willing to do anything to get her to come back to him. He didn't want to lose her ever again.

"Good surf?"

"Great. Are you okay? You look sad." The sadness on her face worried him as he silently prayed she wasn't about to end it.

"I'm fine, just doing some thinking."

Her response didn't fill him with confidence. Sitting down next to her, he noted the first glimmer of the sunrise was beginning and now was the time for what was hopefully a new beginning.

"Will you tell me about James? You don't have to, and I promise to listen and not jump to ridiculous conclusions," he said, still feeling guilty.

There was a moment of silence and Lucas shifted uncomfortably almost ready to tell Montana he didn't need to know and then she spoke.

"James was my husband."

The quiet yet sombre tone she used struck to the heart of him as he felt the world tilt until he fell flat on his face. He never imagined Montana to have been previously married.

"He didn't feel so well so I took him to the hospital and he never came out. H-he died of a massive heart attack at the age of twenty-six," she sobbed, remembering the shock of his death.

Lucas held her tightly, now understanding why she couldn't come inside the hospital when his grandfather was there, and felt so ashamed for not even trying to find out the reason why.

"San Miguel was not only my first holiday in a long time, but my first without James. That's why that day you put lotion on my back, I ran away. James was the last man to ever have done that and I freaked out," she said. "Then I couldn't help but find myself being attracted to you and then felt so guilty about James. How could I possibly have feelings for another man when my husband, the man I supposedly loved, had only been gone for such a short time?"

Lucas could hear the guilt and remorse in her voice and held her tightly, unable to speak because there was nothing he could say to ease it.

"When everyone left and it was just you and me, it felt like, since no one was watching, I could use you to see if I was ready to enjoy a man's company, his touch, a way to start moving on. What I hadn't counted on was falling in love."

His heart burst with song upon hearing her words. She had fallen in love with him from their very first meeting and his world now seemed brighter she felt the same way he had.

"Deep down I knew that doing my OE was really just in hopes of running into you again but we never seemed to be like the others, we didn't seem to agree on what we were and that's what made it hard. Well, that and I still felt guilty about James."

"Why did you never tell me about him?" he said quietly, not in accusation but more for understanding.

"Like I told my friend, Gianni, it was never the right time. First we met and it was a fling and then, well, like I said, we were just bed buddies. It's not something that you share with someone that just flits in and out of your life. You didn't seem to want to get serious and I wasn't sure how to break it to you. I thought you'd freak out and then if or when your family found out, they too, wouldn't be happy that you're dating someone that's already been married and widowed. And besides, we never did really talk about anything deep and meaningful."

Lucas sat there thoughtful. Montana was right. There really never did seem like a right time and they weren't as properly committed as the others. Again guilt assailed him that he'd never bothered to make what he had with her more serious or put in any effort by asking any personal questions.

"So who's Stephen Dobson?" He didn't want to sound jealous but knew this was the man was another unasked question he needed answers to.

"Steve is James' brother. It was a total shock to see him since I hadn't seen him for a long time. He said he's now living in Ireland. Apparently your family invited his boss who couldn't make it after accepting the invite and sent Steve instead," she said.

Lucas felt a huge whack over his head for his own stupidity. If only he hadn't let jealousy rule his emotions, this could have all been cleared up much earlier.

"He came to see me," he said.

"I know. He asked me if I wanted him to tell you the news and I was too chicken to do it myself so I said yes.

She deliberately didn't refer to the baby because she didn't actually know if Stephen told Lucas that bit of information or not and neither had Lucas brought it up.

"You're not a chicken, Mon. You're one of the most bravest and honest people I know, and if only I had taken a leaf out of your book and just asked, none of this would have occurred. I'm the coward," he said, hanging his head.

"Oh Lucas, you're not a coward. I was, for not telling you about James."

"No, you were right, Mon. There never was a right time and once again I'm ashamed I never did bother to get to know you and ask the questions most couples do when getting to know each other," he said. "I've never felt like this before and meeting you, I can safely now say it was love at first sight. Back then, I would have denied it. In fact, I've denied being in love with you all along. I'd probably still be in denial if Stephen hadn't come along and made me face up to it and my mistakes, which I did, and then went back into denial."

"Oh Lucas," she sighed, ecstatic he loved her yet ached for him for his confusion over his feelings. "Did Steve tell you…" Anxiety kicked in as she wasn't sure whether Lucas knew about the baby or not and she worried what he thought if he did know, or how he was going to react if he didn't.

"That you're pregnant?" A bright smile lit up his face instantly putting her at ease. Lucas wasn't angry, he was delighted. His hand went to her stomach and gave it a soothing rub.

"That's what also gave me the kick up my pants to make me stop being stupid and see the truth — that I love you."

"So you didn't think…" Again she was hesitant to ask the question.

"That James was the father? Of course I did. I was still an idiot," he huffed, smiling. "Of course once I got over the shock that *I* was the father, I went to find you, you know."

"You did?" Her eyes were wide with surprise.

Lucas smiled to himself. Indiana, that sneaky little sister, clearly hadn't told Montana he had been there which made his presence here even more unexpected.

"How else would I know that you were here?" he teased.

Montana frowned. It actually hadn't occurred to her to think why Lucas was actually on San Miguel or that he had tried to get in touch with her.

"I don't know. To be honest I haven't even asked myself that question."

"Well, I went to London and met your sister, Indi a few times."

"You did?"

Once again her face was shocked and he grinned.

"She wouldn't even let me in the door. However, I did finally manage to wear her down enough to take pity on me into giving me a clue as to your whereabouts."

"Oh Lucas," she sighed, her heart bursting that he had come to London to talk to her.

"She's a great guard dog. In fact, she wanted us to hurry up and reunite so she and Sofia can travel around Europe on me," he chuckled.

"What?" she shouted, angry at her sister.

"Calm down. I don't mind. It's the least I can do and I know Sofi will not only think that all her luck has come in, but will also take full advantage of my generosity."

"So you're not angry?" she said, unsure if his first answer was the truth.

"At Indi? Of course not."

"No, about me being…pregnant."

"I'm ecstatic, Mon. Unable to believe that you're having my child. It makes me so…" There really weren't enough words but he was very full of love and pride.

She leaned into him needing to be as close him as possible as he wrapped his arms around her and kissed her hair.

"I guess the question is, are you okay with having our child?"

Our child. Two simple words yet encompassed in so much love.

"I couldn't ask for anything better."

He angled her head so he could kiss her with all the love and passion he felt, his heart truly open and bursting knowing Montana would be his wife and the mother of his child.

"You do realise that the others are going to have a heart attack?" he grinned.

"Izzy's going to accuse us of trying to outdo her and then Toni's going to be putting the pressure on Tonio to keep up," she giggled, then turned sober. "Speaking of heart attacks, I wonder if my friend, Gianni has recovered from his?"

Yet another one of Montana's unknown men, he sighed but at least this time he knew to ask anything he wanted to know about Gianni the mystery man. Then another thought struck him like lightning.

"Who's Gianni?"

She couldn't help but giggle at Lucas' seemingly jealous question.

"Don't worry, he's this lovely grandfather I met in the hotel gardens in Rome. In fact, I must have looked like a complete crazy woman when I was demanding the hotel call an ambulance because I thought he was having a heart attack."

"Was he? When was this?" There was a niggling suspicion in his mind that was growing stronger with each moment.

"Oh, it was when you went away for work. I rang the hospital and although they didn't tell me if he did have a heart attack, he was still there when I called so I sent some flowers to hopefully cheer him up."

It wasn't possible, was it? Had Montana inadvertently not only met, but also saved his grandfather's life?

Pulling out his phone from in his bag, he scrolled through some photos before showing her.

"Is this him?"

Montana looked gobsmacked by the photo. There was her friend, Gianni, smiling happily at that camera.

"Yes, that's him. How do you know him?"

"He's my grandfather, Mon. Don't you see, you saved my grandfather's life."

"Oh my God, how is he your grandfather? He said he used to work at the hotel and was missing his wife. I got him cake to cheer him up," she said, stunned by the revelation.

Lucas' laughter broke her concentration.

"What? What's so funny?" she said, confused.

"We own the hotel, so yes, he did used to work there. Why didn't he tell me he met you?" he chuckled, shaking his head at the coincidence, but then sobered. "Oh my God, he did tell me."

"Huh?"

"He told me a story about a woman he met who tragically lost someone she loved at such a young age, and who called for the ambulance and sent him flowers. At the time I wasn't paying too much attention because I was wallowing about you. He was trying to subtly tell me about *you*. Nonno must think I'm an idiot."

"Wow," she said, shaking her head, unable to believe what she just heard. It seemed so far-fetched. "That man, Gianni, is really your grandfather?"

"Yes. You saved my grandfather."

She smiled, tears misting her eyes, knowing that she truly saved someone's life.

"I can't believe it."

"Well, believe it, because you did."

"So now what?" she said, uncertain.

He did what Stephen Dobson suggested and got onto his knees in front of her, tightly holding both her hands.

"I love you, Montana — who's surname I'm ashamed to say that I still don't even know — with all my heart and soul. I'm so ashamed of the way I treated you in Italy. I was so angry that I thought I found the girl of my dreams but when you said in your sleep that you loved James, it absolutely devastated me so I used you for sex. Only you didn't seem to care that I was trying to punish you and that night at the party when I saw you with Stephen, I was so jealous and lost complete control of all my senses, something I've never done before and was disgusted at myself for taking you like that," he said, remorseful.

"Actually, I liked it," she giggled, making him smile.

"If only I had learnt your lesson about being upfront then none of this would ever have happened. You would have told me about James and I wouldn't have been such an idiot. Although in a way, it made me realise just how much I love you," he said, as tears streamed down her face. "Will you be the mother of my children and my love for the rest of our lives? Will you marry me?" His words and tone were so heartfelt and sincere that there was only ever going to be one answer.

"I love you too and yes, I'll marry you, Lucas Romero."

He cupped her face and kissed her so passionately that she was glad she was sitting because she was pretty sure had she been standing, she would have swooned.

Epilogue

After returning from San Miguel, Lucas made sure to reunite Montana with his grandfather, whom she was delighted to see had made a full recovery.

Gianni was overjoyed to not only welcome Montana into the family, but the news she was pregnant made him declare he was feeling better than ever.

The rest of the Romero family were stunned to learn Montana was the one who saved Gianni's life and welcomed her with open arms.

Montana scolded Indi for blackmailing Lucas but he didn't care, he only wanted to win Montana back and was willing to pay any amount, making her look at her fiancé with so much love.

Montana invited Stephen to dinner where Lucas apologised and thanked him for all his help in not only setting him straight, but helping Montana in her hour of need.

Stephen was magnanimous and said that the Dobson family were all delighted Montana had not only moved on with her life, but found love again.

Lucas made it his top priority to make sure Montana looked after herself while he smothered her and the baby with love. Seeing how happy he was she happily let him mother her.

One day as he brought her a plate of lasagne and told her to eat up, she felt a sense of déjà vu.

"What is it?" Lucas said, curious at the wistful look on her face.

Remembering her dreams of James doing the same thing to her, was it possible James sent Lucas to her?

"Nothing. I'm just so happy," she said, looking lovingly at her fiancé.

Seeing him smile back at her with the same love, she ate up all her lasagne.

About the Author

Serena Black's love of reading romance novels, watching soap operas and rom-com TV shows and movies, opened her eyes to a world of romance that could be funny, adventurous, dramatic and sweet.

Now nothing makes her happier than to give readers the same bit of romantic escapism that culminates in happily ever after. No matter where her readers are, whether the day is wet and wintry or one for lazing on the beach, she hopes they pick up a book so that they might laugh, cry or even enjoy the arguments and always close the book with a loud romantic sigh.

Contact Serena at www.serenablackauthor.com.

Coming next:

Indiana's story